The Rumpus Room
and other stories from the suburbs.

Merry Xmas
Josh.
Hope you enjoy
these anecdotal cures
for home sickness
Best
Tim Ross
2017.

The Rumpus Room
and other stories from the suburbs.

1.	The Little House on the Hill	1
2.	The Rumpus Room	16
3.	Newtown Terrace 1999	25
4.	The Shack	33
5.	The First McMansion on the Block	37
6.	The Birth	43
7.	Fremantle Nights	53
8.	The Beach House	61
9.	The Motel	71
10.	New Horizon	77
11.	It's a Shame About Rae's	79
12.	A Couple of Cans on the Back Step	81
13.	The Terrace House Strikes Back	85
14.	The Last Pav	93
15.	Good Night	97

CHAPTER 1

The Little House on the Hill

I always loved the drive home at night, my brothers and I sleepily flopping over each other in the back seat as Dad's old Holden laboured up the long hill that led to our place. An eye would open slightly as Dad's foot slid across the floor of the car and flicked the switch on to high beam. Suddenly the gum trees that hovered across the road lit up like a eucalyptus cave and I felt safe. That hill gave Dad's car quite the work out. The Holden's transmission would stammer then pause and it seemed like a little man under the bonnet with defibrillator paddles would have to scream "Come on you bastard!" to make it to the top. When it felt like it was on its last gasp it heaved, spluttered, finally kicked down a gear and purred as best a Whitlam-era six-cylinder motor could.

Earlier that night at the local pizzeria a man in a singlet with more body hair than five generations of Ross men had cracked an egg on top of some thickly scattered processed ham, slid the family pizza into the oven and then absentmindedly kneaded a mound of dough while watching *Sale of the Century* on a small black and white TV that was surrounded by faded postcards of Rome. It had been my birthday. We'd sat at a pine table, demolished the Aussie pizza and quickly exhausted our maximum two glasses of Solo. Then we rubbed our noses against the freezer cabinet and waited for the man in the singlet to scoop out the gelato. The late night drive home was so familiar it was like a recurring dream. When the car pulled into the carport and the hypnotic motion of the engine ceased we were suddenly awake and traipsed single-file up the stairs into matching pyjamas and straight into bed.

If my parent's generation did something well, apart from buying Rolf Harris records, it was turning bush blocks into suburbs. In the early 1960s they ventured out of inner-city Melbourne and down the Nepean Highway to the fledgling suburb of Mount Eliza. There, a smooth-talking man with a poorly perched toupee took them for a tour through the old dirt tracks to look at bracken-covered sloped blocks studded with bushfire-scarred trees and large boulders of granite that pushed up through the dust like sparkling cysts. The Australian Dream still had a touch of the pioneering spirit in those days and late that afternoon when the sun drew level with his wonky fringe, the man showed them one last block, declaring it the place he would build if he were to retire. Mum and Dad looked down from the side of the mountain through the sea of trees, across the farms of the Moorooduc plains, out on to the blue of Port Phillip Bay and signed on the dotted line.

On a tight budget they built an off-the-rack AV Jennings project home, a simple three-bedroom house on stilts that coped with the slope and made the most of the views. Clad in cedar that seemed to weather and grey in perfect timing with Dad's hair, it was a modest L-shaped house with a mandatory asbestos roof and large aluminum windows across the front-facing lounge room and dining room.

The house touched the earth lightly, built carefully to keep as many of the original gums as possible. Dad obsessed with his bush garden full of natural rocks, grevilleas, kangaroo paws and flowering wattles. Then he turned his hand to a retaining wall for the driveway, made out of bluestone blocks that he scavenged from all over town. Melbourne was modernising and the old bluestone lanes were being ripped up to be replaced by asphalt, so the blocks were free to good homes like ours.

This was the era of being able to do anything yourself, as long as you had a spirit level, a string line and the ability to call out to your next door neighbour when you were trapped under a toppled tank stand. After knocking up the retaining wall Dad set his sights on the area outside the back door. Over the next five years he patiently paved it with assorted blocks of stone and slate that he shaped and cut by hand. It was a work of art; he laid a patchwork of stone waves that wove between the trees, reaching a bluestone circle that he planted out with a large flowering gum. The neighbours were at best confused by his vision and Mum was ambivalent, but I loved it. He found a captive audience in his little blonde-haired kid and I think I may have been the only person who understood what he was trying to achieve.

Across the rest of the garden Dad developed a rather severe addiction to laying mulch and by the late 1970s it had spiralled out of control. The back of his car was constantly full of unlikely materials for the garden bed. First it was seaweed. He had read somewhere that it was a plant super food, which spurred him into action, and he press-ganged us into filling up buckets of the stuff at the beach. There was no time for sunbathing, swimming or beach cricket for the Ross boys — we had mulch to collect. Unfortunately, we must have gathered a variety of seaweed with a high salt content and it killed anything it touched. This was only a temporary setback for Dad and he quickly turned his attention to seedpods. On one of his weekend missions he found a group of native trees along a back road that produced a spiky cone the size of a tennis ball. When he saw there were hundreds of them on the ground he was convinced he'd hit the jackpot. Suddenly we were out of the car madly collecting them. Once the boot was full he had us chucking them on the floor in the back. Just before we jumped in to compete with the flora for some leg room, a familiar orange Datsun pulled up behind us. It was my Year 4 teacher who thought we had broken down.

"No," Dad explained, "We're just collecting pods for the garden." The teacher looked at us blankly, got back into

his 180B and drove off. Thankfully, soon after this incident, Dad lost interest in mulch and the saying 'Families that collect native grevillia pods together, stay together' never made it into general circulation.

Even though the mulch craze had ended, the side of the road continued to be a treasure trove for Dad. On another trip he laid the brakes on in a panic and I was convinced he'd run over a dog. He backed up, jumped out of the car and returned with a pair of denim shorts he'd miraculously spied by the side of the road. He took them home, washed and dried them, tried them on and proudly declared them his new work shorts. They were a little bit loose so he grabbed an occy strap for a belt and for the next five years, whether he was trying to wash the cat with Spray n' Wipe, paint everything he could mission brown or glue his false teeth back together with Araldite, he did it in his work shorts.

There was a wonderful simplicity to the size of our house and I didn't realise how it embraced the practicality of the times until I listened to Australian architect Michael Dysart talk about the project homes he designed in the 1960s. Like our house, the homes he designed at the time had a separate toilet, shower, and a bathroom with a bath and basin. This meant that a family of five could use any of these three rooms separately. Mum could be having a shower, Dad could be putting Cedel hairspray in his hair and my brother could be doing a wee. It's only when you combine all three functions in one room that you need to start building multiple bathrooms in a house.

I often wonder if open plan living would have caught on if they hadn't overcome the issue of electric beaters interfering with the television reception. It used to drive us spare when we were trying to watch *The Goodies* or *Doctor Who* and Mum used to crank up the mixer to make a cake. As soon as she turned it on, the old black and white Kriesler telly used to go into conniptions, static filling the screen and the sound crackling. Those couple of minutes seemed like an eternity and we would yell

at her in the kitchen from our spot on the lounge, demanding her to stop. Today I see the same reaction in my son when the iPad runs out of battery.

It was the bush surrounding the house that gave us our freedom and our place to find adventure. The sprawl was taking its time invading the neighborhood and the empty bush blocks still outnumbered those that had houses by eight to one. The trees all over our mountain were bushfire-scarred and I would trek through them aimlessly with Ted, the little dog that turned up at our house one day and stayed for fifteen years. One of my earliest memories is of lying on the slate path outside the kitchen door and holding Ted's little black and white paw. When I lay on the ground I closed my eyes and mimicked the dog as we shared the joyful warmth of the sun.

One day, walking along one of the bush tracks, I saw two pairs of little brown eyes staring at me. Keeping the always-inquisitive Ted away I moved closer to investigate; a couple of beaks were added and they started squawking. It was a pair of baby tawny frogmouths, two fluffy balls of juvenile owl who had fallen from their nest and forgotten they were supposed to be nocturnal. I ran home to grab Dad and we returned with the ultimate animal welfare device, the cardboard box. The squawks got louder as they bounced down the track and when we got home Dad perched them on the kitchen table and went to work making them some owl food circa 1977. Into a bowl went some creamed honey, Weetbix and milk. Dad mixed it up and slid some straight into their surprisingly wide mouths. They loved it and demanded more. Dad handed me the spoon and I gingerly fed the first one. With growing confidence I lowered the spoon into the box and the second one, hungrier than the first, lunged at the spoon and it caught in its beak. I panicked and let go, momentarily thinking I'd choked our new little friend, but it just shook its head a few times and the spoon flew out.

Tawny frogmouths are often called mopokes because of the distinctive sound they make. So Dad named them Poke and Mopoke. They seemed quite happy living in their box on the balcony and eating Sanitarium health food products three times a day. The dog Ted had given them a sniff, found them largely boring and didn't give them a second look. Within a week they become more active and we pulled them out of the box and let them run around the balcony. As they gained confidence they started flapping their wings up and down and we'd stand on the sidelines and will these balls of fluff to get up enough speed and momentum so they could fly. It took them a couple of days but they finally managed to get a bit of air and then one evening at dusk an adult tawny frogmouth turned up on the balcony. Poke and Mopoke suddenly hopped out of the box and made a run for it like a couple of spitfires taking off for the Battle of Britain and off they went with their Mum into the night. A month

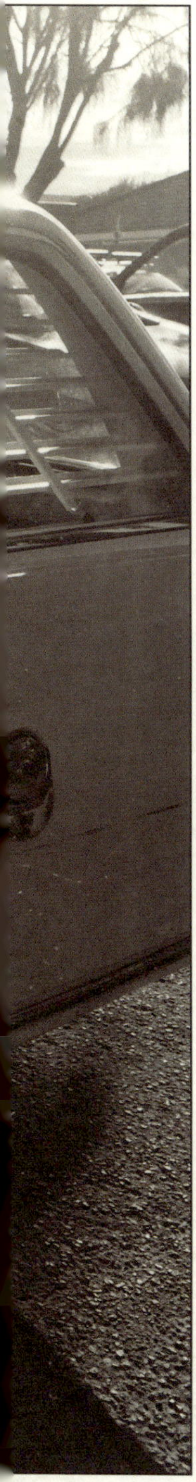

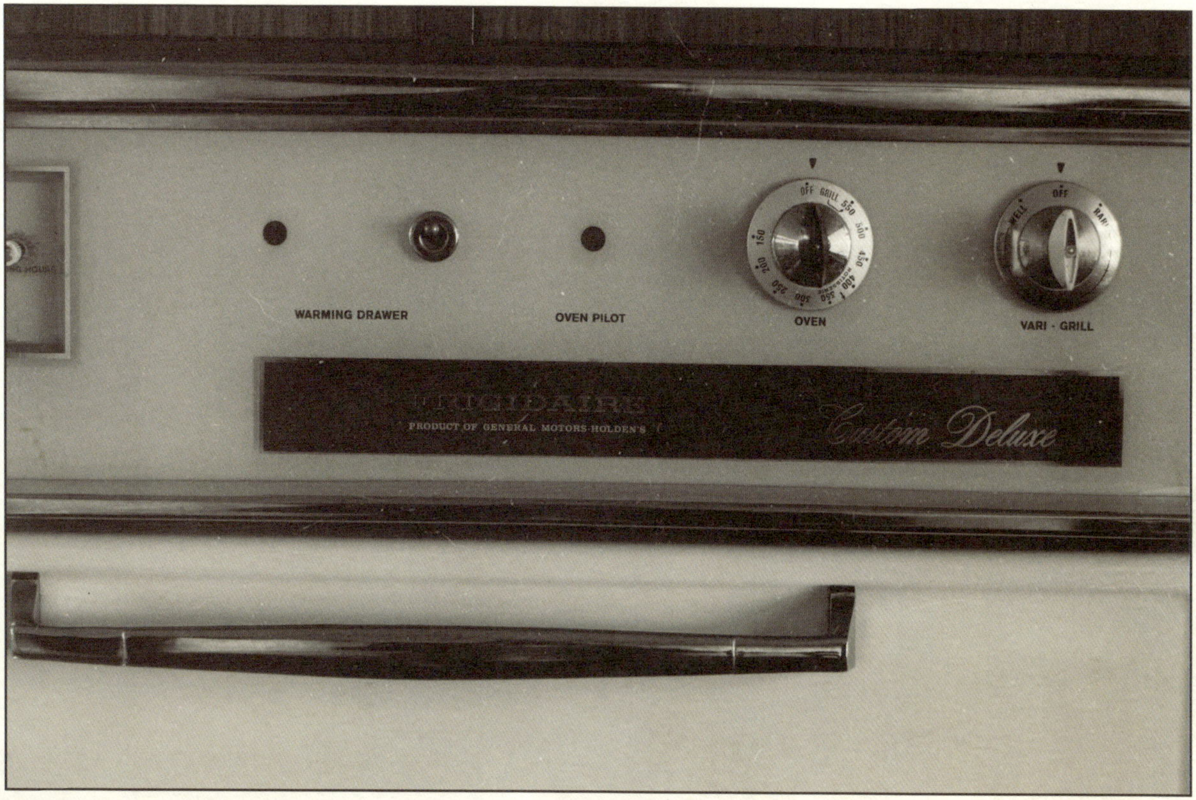
WARMING DRAWER
OVEN PILOT
OVEN
VARI - GRILL
FRIGIDAIRE
PRODUCT OF GENERAL MOTORS-HOLDEN'S
Custom Deluxe

later they arrived back fully grown and perched themselves on the verandah balustrade just the outside the lounge room. Excited to see them I rushed out and they happily let me give them a pat. Dad joined us and gave them half a raw sausage each, which they demolished, and then they flew off and never returned. For years whenever I saw a tawny frogmouth at night I always wondered whether they were related to my little friends.

One day a For Sale sign went up on the block next door to where I found the owls. There was an auction where my folks got involved in some spirited bidding with nobody and ended up with a piece of land that was to become our tennis court. It only took five years to actually start the process, which involved Dad paying some blokes who were working on the roads not very much on the side to bulldoze a few trees and excavate into the hill to level up the area for the court. Dad, using his non-existent engineering degree, got the guys to make a retaining wall by stacking the large trees they knocked over and then they backfilled it with all the soil and clay they had taken from the excavation. They graded it a bit but the job of actually making the whole area properly level was left in the capable hands of the Ross boys with the finest machinery and tools — a shovel, rake and wheelbarrow. For a couple of weeks during the Christmas holidays we were like an underage chain gang moving soil around, all under the promise of one day being able to play tennis at home.

In what was a surprise to everyone, not least the old man, we actually managed to level it off to the point that a tennis court be put on the block. This is where proceedings stalled. I wasn't fussed because I didn't have much interest in playing. I'd been sent off to lessons at the house of a friend of our neighbour's who had an unregistered coaching business on the side. He had a washing basket full of balls and a beard like GI Joe and this seemed enough qualification for most parents. Despite complaints about him being a little too hands-on with some of his female teenage clients, he had a roaring business. On Saturday mornings he had back-to-back lessons and while waiting for mine I tried a new aluminum racket one of my friends had just been given. I myself had an old racket from the sixties which featured the signature of an Australian Davis Cup player nobody had ever heard of. It was extremely heavy and my little arms had a lot of trouble lifting it up to play shots

properly. The new racquet was much easier for me to swing, so I grabbed a banana passionfruit off the large vine that was growing against the side of the house and lobbed one straight over into next door. It landed splat on the neighbour's car, a complaint was made and everyone in a twenty metre radius happily dobbed on me, so I was banned from further lessons.

There was never any more work done on our tennis court, a familiar story in our house. One winter our central heating went on the blink and for the next five years we tried to keep the house warm with the open fire and one electric oil heater. When Mum finally did get someone out to take a look, it took the repairman all of fifteen seconds to work out that the pilot light had gone out. We weren't as bad as the Kennedys up the road though. In the middle of 1985 they bought a new wall oven and put it in the lounge room in readiness to replace the old one. I am told that the oven is still sitting in its box in the lounge room today with a doily and a maidenhair fern on top.

We all have a fascination with our childhood homes. They seemed much bigger when we were kids, just like our schools did. I recently went back inside that old house for the first time in twenty years with mixed emotions. I was curious to see how it looked but also reticent to potentially unlock some emotions that had been bubbling beneath for some time. From the outside the house was completely unrecognisable. The cedar boards had been ripped off and replaced with cement sheeting that was covered with a decorative coating and painted a shade of mid-nineties Tuscan yellow. Inside was also unrecognisable. The floor plan was largely the same but I didn't feel anything walking around. It was like I was trying to pull memories out of the place, but nothing budged. They had turned my old room into the master bedroom and added an ensuite. Bizarrely, Dad's old workshop where he tinkered and repaired things was now a fully fledged teppanyaki bar.

This house could not have been more different than the one I grew up in. It was like walking past an old girlfriend that I didn't recognise. The only things that remained were a bluestone retaining wall and a large granite boulder on the surprisingly still-spare block next door. I used to sit on that boulder and wait for Mum and Dad to come home from work. Ted the dog always jumped up on the rock with me — he loved the vantage point — and as I sat down on the rock when I returned all those years later I swear I could feel him brushing up against me. Our little home was gone but the ghost of the old dog was still there. Later that day I told a friend how I felt the dog's presence and she put it simply and perfectly: "Sounds like he was glad to see you."

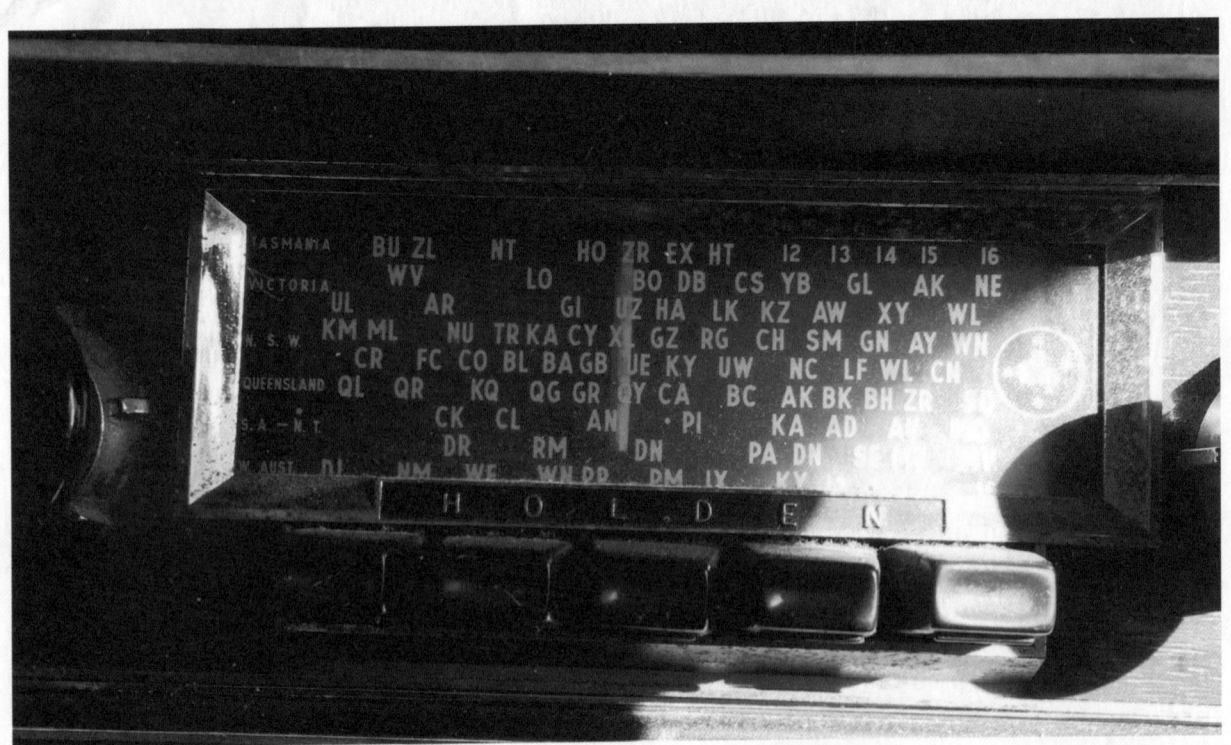

CHAPTER 2

The Rumpus Room

It was during the summer of 1979 when one of Mum's colleagues invited us over for a family barbecue and we felt like we had walked straight on to the set of the American TV show *Hart to Hart**. They had a sprawling Hamptons-style white timber home surrounded by a row of sculpted hedges, manicured lawns and perfectly formed oak trees. As we pulled into the driveway, parking the family Kingswood behind the shiny red Mercedes convertible, we all sat wide-eyed while Dad muttered something about it looking like the sort of place they filmed pornos.

Inside we met a family with clean, fluffy seventies hair, sparkling teeth and golden tans. The McRichfucks had three kids, all around our ages but twice as good looking. The oldest at fourteen was parading around in a bikini and sun visor and carrying a Yonex tennis racket. She had two younger brothers who had the same confidence, but weren't wearing bikinis. They called their parents by their first names and happily led us into their Rumpus Room while the adults went out to the pool to eat cashews and drink Moselle.

The Rumpus Room can be described in two ways: the one you had and the one you wished you had. I don't know whether they are around as much today, but in the golden years of absent parenting they ruled supreme. In simple terms they were a room designed for kids to hang out in while their parents wore clothes made of synthetic fibres and experimented with drink driving.

The McRichfucks' Rumpus Room had chocolate shag pile carpet and green velvet curtains that had been thrown open so we could cop a view of the large sparkling pool and Dad standing around in a pair of powder blue Simpson tennis shorts. It had a ping-pong table, a colour TV and a shelf containing what looked like every board game ever invented, including the one we all coveted, Test Match.

We had inherited the original (and crappier) version of this game from our grandfather. You opened the lid of the box to reveal a couple of cardboard wheels that were rotated by a small brass tack-like handle. After pushing them back and forth, it would show you the outcome of every 'ball' being 'bowled'. Given that it was invented in a time when people were aroused by the concept of eating bread and dripping there is no surprise that it was a pretty ordinary game.

The second incarnation was far more high-tech. It involved laying a piece of green felt on the floor for the oval and placing your small cricket figurines all around the 'ground'. A ball bearing was placed in a lever on the bowler's arm and released towards the batsman figurine that had its own lever attached to the bat. Pulling it back would smack the ball bearing towards the boundary, hopefully avoiding the fieldsmen who had a U-shaped plastic receptacle molded between their legs. If the ball did go there, you were 'caught' and therefore out. As dinky as this sounds, if you had one of these in the late seventies or early eighties you were more popular with your friends than Joel Garner at an over twenty-eight's nightclub. Apparently they still make them today and I presume the only people who buy them are those who desperately wanted one in their youth but never got one.

*Google it

Our quandary was what to play with first. We felt like we were in the games room at a resort. The only Rumpus Room I'd seen that came close to rivalling it belonged to a kid I'd met through the cricket club. Brian was an only child whose family lived in an orange brick house at the bottom of a court. His parents had converted half of the double garage into his Rumpus Room. The brick was covered with wood veneer panelling and a dark brown timber bar in the corner contained a bar fridge stacked with mini cans of soft drink. Cat hair-covered lime green beanbags were placed on the seagrass matting floor and not only did he have his own colour TV and stereo, but also his own pinball machine. Brian may have been lucky to have his own pinnie parlour in the garage, but not so lucky with his teeth, which were severely bucked. This led him to be known as Headjob Jaws around the club, but when he finally received orthodontic treatment it didn't help his cause. He then copped the new nickname, Brace Fellate Face, which was equally as cruel but much harder to say.

His new moniker came courtesy of Banksy, one of the finest junior psychopaths in the history of the club. Banksy had once carried a large rock up a ladder and on to the roof of his two-story house and then called his older brother to come outside. When he walked out the door, Banksy, standing above him waiting, dropped the rock directly on to his head. Luckily it didn't kill him — he was only mildly concussed and had enough faculties to get up the ladder and try and throttle him. Banksy waited until he got on to the roof and was lunging towards him before he crazily leaped two metres to the hanging branch of a gum, scampered down the trunk at lightning pace and ran round and removed the ladder, leaving his brother stranded. Somehow his brother finally managed to lower himself down the side of the house and when he got his hands on Banksy he bound and gagged him with rope and left him in a one metre-deep trench that had just been dug to lay new pipes. He then grabbed his bike and went off to a mate's place for the night. It wasn't until his Mum came home from work seven hours later and saw his head bobbing up and down from the trench desperately trying to scream that Banksy was finally set free.

As for Brian, at the start of Year 7 his family and the pinball machine moved south to Hobart when his Dad decided to open a squash court on the Apple Isle. Fifteen years later I was driving down St Kilda Road and saw him carrying a cricket bag and eating a souvlaki. I couldn't help but wonder what had happened to his pinball machine.

They may not have had arcade games but after half an hour of being beaten in ping pong by my brother, the McRichfucks kicked things up a notch when the daughter walked into the Rumpus Room carrying a bucket of Kentucky Fried Chicken. I'm pretty sure I'd only ever seen a bucket full of chicken on ads on the telly.

One of my school friends' Mums, who had a full-length poster of Elvis in his white jumpsuit hanging in the lounge room, used to make a homemade version that involved dipping Chicken Marylands into beaten egg, covering them in Cornflakes and then popping them in the oven. I can't imagine that a Kelloggs breakfast cereal was one of the Colonel's eleven secret herbs and spices, and true enough, her chicken tasted remarkably like chicken with cornflakes stuck to it.

While we munched our way through the bucket, only pausing to wipe our greasy hands on the carpet, the boys showed us the art of eating just the crunchy skin and leaving the meat on the bones. In the end there was large pile of skin-stripped pieces sitting next to the used refresher towelettes, an item we found as novel as the bucket of chicken itself. Before we knew it, the day was over and we piled into the car and went home. I can't remember being invited to the McRichfucks' again. Probably it was the grease stains we left on the shag pile carpet.

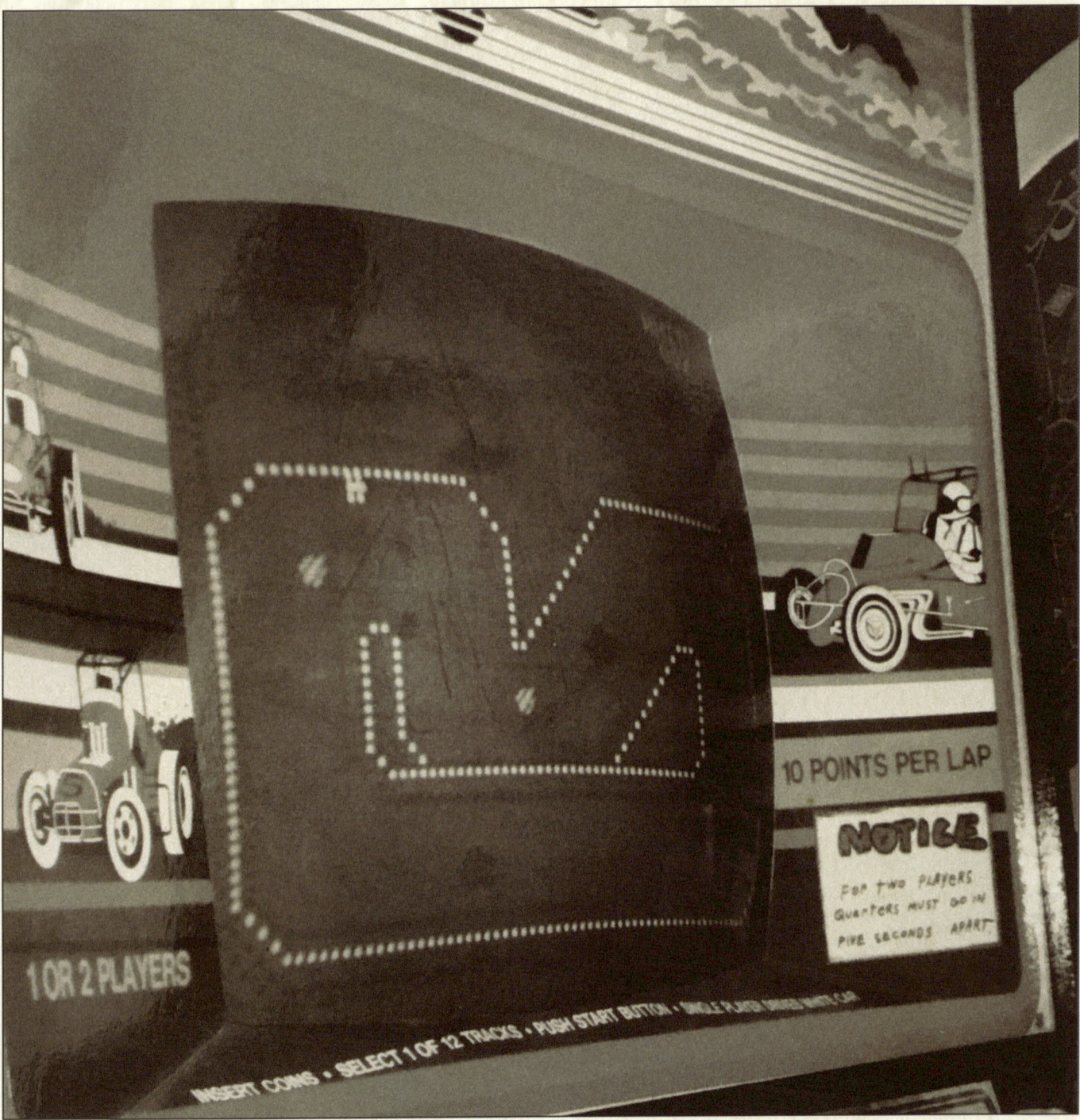

The great Rumpus Rooms always had either a ping pong table or a pool table. We had neither; we had a thing called a bobs set. Sure, it had balls and a cue, but the rest of it was just a slender half-metre long wooden box that had ten numbered arches across the front. You played by shooting the balls along the floor and through the arches. It was entertaining enough as a game, but not one that was ever up for Olympic consideration. In the corner we had an old black and white TV that needed pliers to switch it on, except there was no point as we didn't have an aerial in the room. Rounding out the fun palace was an out-of-tune piano, mum's sewing machine and the ironing board. This was the real dark secret of our rumpus room — although it was called the Rumpus Room or the End Room (because it was at the end of the house), in reality it was really the ironing room. Was it any wonder we sought our jollies in the homes of others? I once continued to date a girl in high school largely because her parents seemed to have a never-ending supply of sliced salami in their fridge. Although it was a strange and shallow reason to continue a romance, there were only Saladas with Vegemite at home.

The best Rumpus Room I ever saw was at the end of summer at the start of 1982. I was in my first year of high school and I had quickly become friends with Karl. He, like a girl called Sonia who was also in my year, somehow managed to have nicotine-stained teeth from a heavy year of smoking in Year 6. Sonia wore a shark's tooth necklace and had an unusual crush on her brother (a recent check on Facebook confirms that she didn't marry her brother but the teeth are still yellow. No mention of the necklace).

Karl's crooked yellow teeth and sideways smile contributed to his roguish bogan charm that seemed so prevalent at the time. He had a black East Coast windcheater with the sleeves cut off above the elbow and wore tight blue stretch Faberge jeans. I was wearing my brother's hand-me-down grey Levi Californians, which had a freshly out-of-date flare, so his style was a revelation.

We used to catch the school bus together and one afternoon he invited me back to his place. Situated on a large gum-treed block on a dead-end avenue, his house was a classic split-level brick veneer Australian home. It had a brown tile roof, mission brown windows, beams and doors, and red clinker brick walls. The sloping garden was held back with railway sleeper retaining walls that were planted out with grevilleas and native creepers. At the back of the house a brick courtyard with a timber pergola led to an in-ground Pebblecrete pool. As soon as we topped up on red cordial, Karl lent me a pair of his boardies and we started doing bombs in the pool. When his brother came home the three of us played cricket with a tennis ball with electrical tape attached to one side. Doing this meant that when we bowled, the ball swung away from the outside edge of their twin scooped cricket bat and into the metal bin/automatic wicket keeper. His brother Derrick was wildly uncoordinated yet had the swagger of a fifteen year old, with a full set of pubes well before his peers. He would rearrange his boardies to show the pubes off just before taking his stance to bat.

We had a gravel driveway at home so I loved the novelty of bowling on a concrete pitch. Time and time again with the aid of the tape I managed to get the ball past his probing bat and my hand shot up at the sound of that familiar bang of the ball hitting the metal wicket. For years most forms of backyard cricket had been traditionally stacked in favour of the batsmen and even rules like six-and-out and one-hand-one-bounce couldn't do much to even the scales. I once bowled at my brother for three hours on a thirty-five degree day without getting him out, but the advent of electrical tape on a tennis ball changed backyard cricket forever. Karl got sick of me getting him out and dragged me back inside. We went through the kitchen, which had a large yellow laminate benchtop hanging between two brick pylons. Karl's Mum was sitting at the bench having an animated conversation with a friend on the white push button phone attached to the kitchen wall. We slid past as she rocked back and forth on a pine stool with a plastic goblet of white wine in hand. I wasn't much of an eavesdropper but it was hard not to overhear her describing someone called Neil as a 'total cunt'.

We went down a set of light brown-carpeted stairs and Karl opened a pair of sliding doors to reveal their Rumpus Room. It had a pool table on one side and on the other was a dark brown cord couch and two matching armchairs that surrounded a large Rank Arena TV. Under the TV were a VCR player and not one, but two, video game consoles — the two biggest ones on the market at the time, Atari and Intellivision. As I sat there on the couch, the smell of chlorine and their accumulation of consumer electronics was intoxicating. I was prepared to sit in this perfect room and play video games for eternity. Karl was rifling through the game cartridges ready to fire up one of the machines when the doorbell rang. Mum had arrived to pick me up. I was devastated. I hadn't even had the opportunity to play one game of Moon Patrol. There was a small glimmer of hope when Karl's Mum, standing there in her white one-piece, waved a bottle of Chardonnay around but unfortunately Mum declined and I was out of the door quicker than you could say "Neil's a total cunt".

The next day, Karl invited me to sleep over at his place that Friday night. That meant I'd be hanging out in their Rumpus Room playing video games and watching movies all Friday night and Saturday morning. We had no such excitement at our place; the most radical thing my mates might experience when they slept over was the dog almost choking on a chop bone. It's not that I wanted to have wall-to-wall video games at our house. I didn't need a clairvoyant to tell me that in no time in the next three years would the folks roll in fresh from Myer with an Atari 2600 wrapped in a bow. We weren't great consumers, it wasn't in our makeup, and that made experiencing these things in other people's homes more exciting. If by some incredible fluke we did actually end up with a pool table and a tabletop Space Invaders machine it wouldn't have felt right. It would have been like going to the Deb Ball with your sister… not that I went to a Deb Ball or had a sister.

The fascination was that things were actually different in other people's homes. It was the beginning of the inkling that I was marooned in the suburbs. I, like many kids of the 'burbs, found that the thing I loved most about the bush blocks — the wide open space — was becoming more isolating as I grew up. The lure of the city loomed large. The suburbs gave us the freedom to roam but there was monotony in knowing what was at the end of the street and around the corner. In the pre-internet, pre-cable days our sources of information were limited. On the telly, blandness ruled supreme. Can you imagine a whole family sitting down today to watch something as terrible as *The Love Boat*? There'd be a mutiny. We had the radio, the newspaper and a certain amount of books in the house, and we always had the library, but there was a reason we would read the back of a cereal box — there was nothing else to do. In the iPad age, there isn't a kid today who could tell you what niacin is but in 1983 I could recite the ingredients of Nutri-Grain without blinking.

Friday could not have come soon enough and it was almost an exact replay of three days before. We jumped off the pergola into the pool and I once again had Derrick in all sorts with the electrical-taped ball. Karl's mum was still swanning around the house in her white one-piece and she even managed to put some frozen pizza subs in the oven for us without having to put down her glass of wine. Making the most of what remained of the light, we held off having any serious time in the Rumpus Room to continue our cricket session. I had just opened up my shoulders and tonked one of Derrick's pedestrian outswingers long and high across the road and into the neighbor's rhododendrons. A despondent Derrick turned round to fetch the ball as a silver Holden Statesman pulled into the driveway. The door opened and out jumped a forty-five year old man in a lemon pair of slacks and an orange short-sleeve shirt with a sunset motif on the back. He had a medium-length early-eighties moustache, a gold chain dangling on a fully carpeted chest and slightly thinning brown hair that was parted to the side.

Karl and Derrick ran over to their Dad and gave him a hug. Karl introduced me to him and like all great Dads of the era he shook my hand and promptly forgot my name. He had a gold bracelet dangling on his wrist and smelt of Winfield Blues. He sauntered into the house, every inch the Frankston South Magnum P.I., and suddenly I realised that he didn't live in the house and, more tellingly, this was 'Neil'. I can only surmise about the list of marital misdemeanors that Neil had on his rap sheet but I'm guessing bringing home gonorrhea rather than a family-size pizza may have been right at the top.

I was interested in continuing my innings at the crease but the brothers wanted to hang out with their Dad. When we were inside, Mum in the one-piece was giving Neil a piece of her mind. We kept moving and went out by the pool and within

minutes Mum in a one-piece called Karl inside. When he came back out he explained that his Dad had made an unscheduled visit to see them and that his Mum wouldn't let him stay in the house. I had a few choices: I could stay in the house with Mum in a one-piece, go home, or jump in the Statesman and stay with them and his Dad. It was all completely strange and before I knew it we were in the back of the car listening to Dr. Hook and enjoying some secondhand cigarette smoke. I don't think any attempt was made to tell my parents that I was on Neil's Magical Mystery Tour and after driving a few kilometres up the road we pulled off the highway into a budget motel. This was when I realised that we weren't staying at Neil's house. I didn't ask Karl why we were staying in a motel or where his Dad actually lived. Neil checked in, organised a couple of extra fold-out beds and went next door to get some takeaway Chinese. I sat on my bed and ate sweet and sour pork while we all watched *Sons and Daughters* on telly. When it finished Neil turned off the lights and I lay there staring at the ceiling trying to get pineapple out from between my teeth.

CHAPTER 3
Newtown Terrace 1999

It took Dane two days to realise he'd caught scabies from the 1970s lumber jacket he bought at Glebe Markets. It cost him fifty bucks and he was unsure of it when he tried it on, but the girl with the henna tats and Byron Bay smile talked him into it. He'd only ducked into her vintage clothes stall to avoid his ex-housemate Megan.

Megan had called a house meeting (even though there was only the two of them) and asked him to move out because of his excessive drinking. He didn't think he'd been drinking any more or less than usual. Then again, he'd just retired his tight Bonds t-shirts because of his growing mini volcano titties and mid-twenties gut.

Although he protested at first, he could see that the feisty art student with her nose ring and obsession with Ani DiFranco wasn't going to back down anytime soon. He packed up his single mattress, took the fridge, his guitar and amp and moved to a run-down one-bedroom terrace house in Newtown. His sister had been living in the terrace for the last five years and threw him the lease when she decided to leave her boyfriend and move to Melbourne to find herself. She found herself within a week, right on top of the lead singer of Fitzroy Funk band. He liked to juggle skittles on stage and pretend that he didn't have herpes. Nobody was quite sure which was worse.

Dane found himself almost living alone for the first time since he moved out of the family home in suburban Bexley two years ago. He had expected his Mum to be devastated, but shouldn't have worried. No sooner had he pulled his geriatric yellow Camira out of the driveway than his Mum rented his room out to an overseas student. Next time he visited home, the student was sitting on the couch wearing his old HSC windcheater, eating a banana Paddle Pop and calling his Mum, Mum. Dane was ropable; she never had Paddle Pops in the freezer when he was living there.

He was now sharing the Newtown house with Mugsy, his sister's cat. Mugsy was gold, brown and white and had a bell around his neck. Mugsy didn't get the email about moving to Melbourne and the heartbroken ex-boyfriend couldn't cope with keeping him. Every time Mugsy took a shit in his tray, it reminded him of her. And Mugsy was a prolific shitter, so the pain was immense.

Dane quickly found a soft spot for the cat. They grew closer when Mugsy became addicted to licking the scabies lotion off Dane's legs, which he applied twice a day for a week. Mugsy didn't seem to have an adverse reaction. But the real bonding time between man and cat came when Dane found out the real reason that Megan had kicked him out.

One Tuesday afternoon he had popped into the Annandale Hotel to grab a copy of the street press to see whether they'd published a review of his band's debut EP 'More Leisure Than Pleasure'. The cover featured the guys wearing matching ladies velour tracksuits they'd found in Kmart. While he fruitlessly flicked through the pages, Megan's brother Phil walked into the pub lugging a Marshall amp. He joined Dane for a schooner and within minutes Dane knew what he had done. Apparently after a sizeable evening at the Marlborough Hotel he had gone home and decided to watch one of his old pornos in the lounge room. When Megan came home an hour

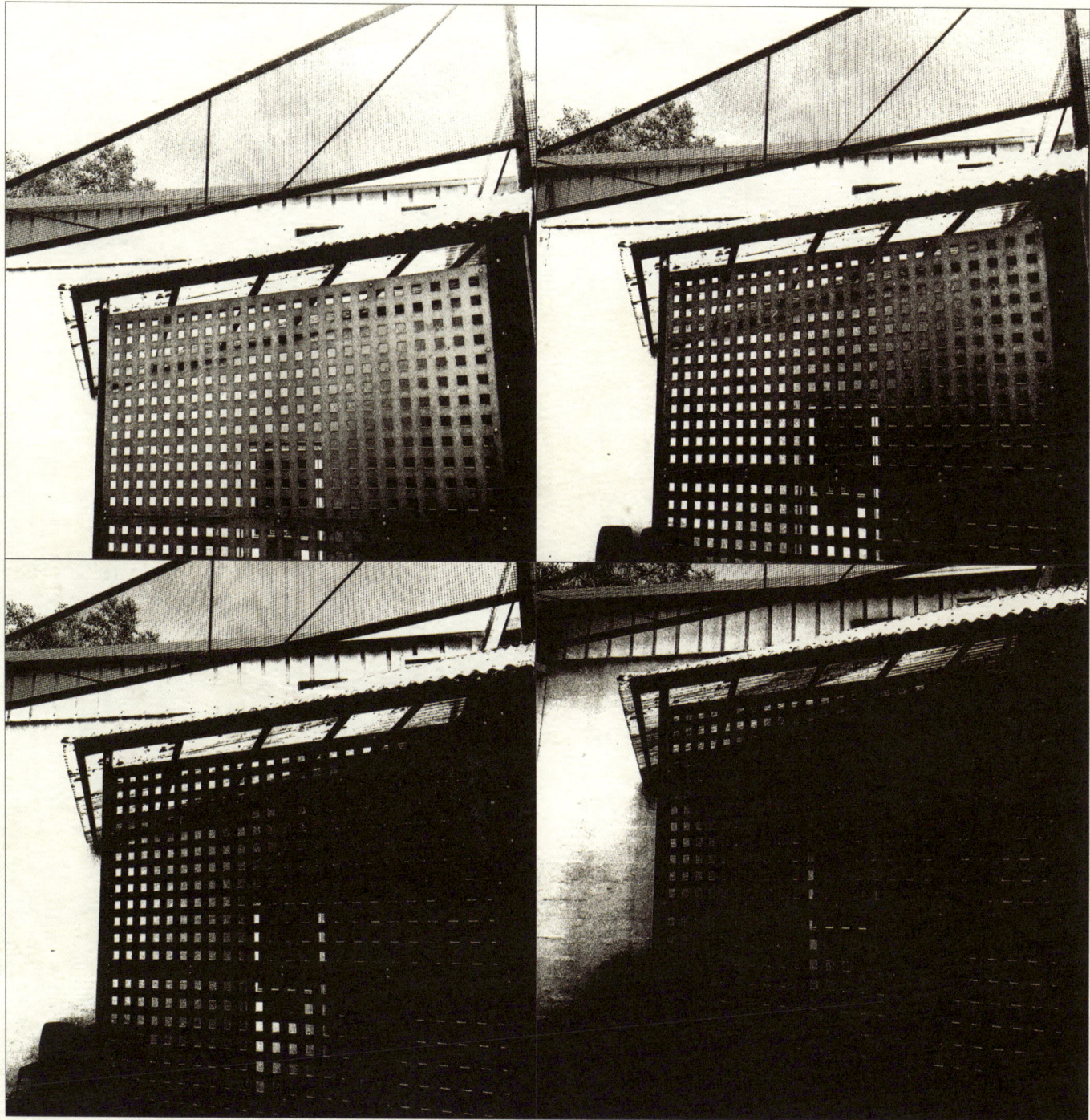

later she walked in and found him passed out on the couch with his rust-coloured cords around his ankles, his limp penis lying exposed and a bottle of Crisco vegetable oil sitting on the coffee table. Dane always wanked with Crisco, so he knew it was true. He asked Phil if everyone knew the story. The answer was yes and he was now known as The Crisco Kid. He decided it was time to take shelter with Mugsy and didn't leave the house for a week.

Deeply embarrassed, he lobbed the vegetable oil in the bin and banned himself from masturbating. It lasted at least three hours. He sat on the couch with his guitar and tried to write songs but was overcome with the thought of everyone laughing at him. The little cat was both a great distraction and some well-needed company. He knew that he could live for a week without going to uni but could he last a week talking only to a cat?

The answer was yes. Mugsy was without judgement and as long as his bowl of Go Kat on the kitchen floor was refilled a couple of times a day he was happy. Mugsy would follow him around rubbing himself on Dane's legs, looking up at him and pretending to know what he was talking about. The only place he would never go was the bedroom. He would sit at the door but never enter. When Dane picked him up and tried to physically bring him in, Mugsy went ballistic. He scratched and screeched until Dane let go and he fucked off down the stairs and hid in the bathroom.

Dane killed the time watching TV and sleeping. Totally paranoid, he set his clock radio to wake him at 2am every morning so he could sneak out unseen and go to the servo on Parramatta Road for supplies. His Mum had rung just the once but he let it go to voicemail. She had only wanted to know where his cricket bat was. The student had been watching the one-dayers on TV and was keen to give it a go. At least she hadn't heard the story.

After a week he was slowly going insane and decided he needed to face the world. The safest first step was band practise. He walked into their rehearsal studio and there was a packet of frozen crinkle cut chips sitting on top of his amp.

"Excuse me guys, I'm off for a wank."

Everyone laughed and they moved on. Two days later at the Town Hall Hotel he somehow found himself talking to an attractive girl with brown hair. She seemed oblivious to his styvo breath and the Reschs stains on his Western shirt. They'd broken

off from the crowd and perched themselves on the padded swivel chairs in the pokies room, chatting to the annoying jingly soundtrack of the Queen of The Nile machine. She was attentive and interested, a hurricane swirl of everything brown and pretty: eyes, hair and freckles.

This wasn't a normal situation for him. Most times he met anyone at this hotel it had been at the dirty end of the night and it was only drunken circumstantial loneliness that brought them together. He had become comfortable with the mutual mild revulsion of the needy 5am hook up. Like magnets forcing off each other, pimply skin jarred against flab, overgrown pubes barked at each other and eye contact was avoided at all costs. Bodies were used all fast and furious until the magnets flipped and connected and regret ejaculated, just as the sun rose over King Street and beyond. Someone always left without saying goodbye.

This was different; there was actually an attraction. She told him about her spiritual side and how she made a living doing readings. No, she didn't have an actual crystal ball but yes, she was pretty much accurate. She had always been able to converse with people's spirit guides. No, she didn't want to give him a reading. He didn't want to be cynical, he wanted her too much.

They talked until closing and, without discussing it, found themselves walking back to his place. He thought he would sing 'Heavy Heart' to her on his acoustic guitar but decided not to be a fuckwit. He poured them both a glass of beer, which they barely touched. Instead they let the old brown vinyl couch cling to them while they made out and Mugsy jumped all over them. This gave Dane the perfect reason to suggest continuing upstairs; he told her how Mugsy refused to go in to his room.

They went up and it happened with considerable frenzy. When it was light and they finally decided to get some sleep, he knew she wouldn't leave without saying goodbye. When they woke it was 2pm. She told him that the reason Mugsy wouldn't come in was because there was a spirit present. The spirit was friendly but she was happy to move him on if he liked. He was intrigued. He wanted to see whether it would work and told her to go for it. He got up and went to the bathroom and when he returned Mugsy was sitting on the bed licking his paws. Dane was impressed.

She had to go. She was going to Newcastle for a spiritual festival but would be back next week and they could hang out then. She kissed him goodbye. Dane lay on the bed with Mugsy and smiled and smiled. Hungover but happy he went downstairs to get himself and the cat a feed. Mugsy followed but stopped at the kitchen door. Dane poured Go Kat into his bowl but he didn't budge. It seemed she had only moved the spirit on as far as the kitchen.

CHAPTER 4

The Shack

It was the holiday where I learnt how to be properly paranoid for the very first time. It was also the holiday where we found out Elvis had died.

Our beach holidays traditionally happened in winter when the rent was considerably cheaper. Mum always found a house through someone we knew. Such-and-such with the glass eye at church knew so-and-so with a lazy eye and they had some little place at a beach that was nowhere near the Gold Coast. The August that the King kicked the bucket, we headed off to a place the owners called The Shack at Waratah Bay.

Today the notion of the shack is a romantic one. It conjures up images of comfortable, worn sofas covered in woollen throws; open fires, home-made shelves displaying jars full of old shells, rustic fishing baskets and artfully arranged bird's nests. This Shack didn't have any driftwood tied together with rope to make a pendant lamp, nor did it have scented candles on a stack of vintage books. This was the sort of shack that some drunken old man of the sea had nailed together with things that he'd stolen from building sites. The only thing rustic was the selection of rat traps that were scattered on the battered lino kitchen floor.

We were pretty used to staying in wonky old houses but even Mum knew this place was shit. It didn't sit elegantly in the dunes like something out of a coffee table book, but flatly on a small clearing amongst some tea trees. The almost windowless corrugated iron structure looked like more like an oversized site dunny than a relaxing holiday home. It had two bedrooms, one with a small metal-framed double bed and the other with two bunk beds that were so unstable they had been chained to the exposed stud wall to stop them toppling over when you climbed up the ladder. It would have been dream accommodation if you'd just been shipwrecked and had resorted to eating raw seagulls for tea.

It didn't take us long to realise we could be reasonably comfortable if we had the wood stove going full bore twenty-four hours a day and if we walked around wrapped in our doonas. The Shack didn't have a TV, or even a lounge room, so at night we sat at the laminate table and played cards, mostly

500. It was here in the kitchen that we heard on the radio that Elvis had died. Nobody was overly affected by the news. Mum dealt the cards again then picked up her knitting and Dad called Eight No Trumps.

To take a break from the cards one night, Dad drove us in to the town to see a local theatre group production of a Charlie Brown musical. We sat in the local hall on fold-up chairs eating Minties and waited for the show to start. When the curtain finally opened we were greeted by a plump middle-aged woman playing Lucy, then Linus came on stage played by a plump middle-aged woman and then Charlie Brown… you get the drift. Despite the menopausal overacting and bad American accents we all rather enjoyed the gas heating in the hall and it was deemed a successful night. Sure it didn't reach the dizzying heights of the two-hour documentary on soil erosion we'd watched the year before in a Mechanics Hall in Inverloch, but at least we were out of The Shack.

Mum had found a magazine recipe for pizza that used potato in the dough and could be cooked in the electric frypan, a concept that even today would make Australians excited. Once a month we would have Family Teas at the church and almost everyone would bring their dish in an electric frypan. We'd all line up at a trestle table for a mega Christian buffet of savoury mince, beef goulash and five different types of casseroles flavoured by canned or packet soup.

The potato in the dough wasn't exactly potato, it was Deb; dehydrated potato flakes in a packet. As a rule, Mum wasn't a fan, but had made an exception because it was school holidays and we deserved a treat. The base actually worked quite well and tasted much more like pizza than the other popular method in our house — microwaved Lebanese bread covered with tomato paste and grated tasty cheese. My poor brother Campbell accidentally spilt his glass of strawberry Nesquik all over his slice. Dad swapped plates and did a terrible job of pretending that the milk-soaked slice had developed a sweet and sour quality that tasted rather gourmet.

On the small bookshelf amongst well-thumbed *Australasian Post* magazines I found a book called *Deadly Australian Creatures*. I read it from cover to cover and became obsessed with all the things that could potentially kill or harm me on the holiday. I'd lay in the bottom bunk at night while my brothers were asleep and talk myself into the awful truth that I wouldn't make it through the next day without being attacked by at least one of the creatures from the book.

I was certain that when I went outside to grab some logs for the fire that a redback spider would be waiting, ready to pounce, and I would be powerless to stop it. I managed to move on from that scenario by replacing it with one where I would step on a hibernating brown snake who was so angry that I'd woken him from his slumber that he ripped straight through my gumboots. That scenario finished with me applying a tourniquet and hoping they had the antivenom at the local hospital. The next horror fantasy was bush tics; I'd pat a local dog who was carrying them and the next day would wake up paralysed and spend the rest of my life in a wheelchair.

The more paranoid I got, the more I kept flicking through the book and the more my mind raced completely out of control. The page featuring the blue-ringed octopus told how they often lived in old soft drink cans and small children had been known to pick up a can in a rockpool, put their finger in the hole and practically die on the spot. Logically I imagined that any empty can of soft drink could have a killer lurking inside, it didn't even need to be at the beach. What if someone grabbed a can off the beach and took it to the Cash-A-Can centre, and when we dropped off some cans, I accidentally picked up that can, and the octopus, who had always been a water-hater and was digging his new life, grabbed my finger and sent me off in a body bag?

The fear and paranoia kept creating extra layers of tension and it wasn't until I walked past a guy welding a fence and I was sure I was going to go blind looking at the flame that I finally broke down to Mum and Dad and let them know the terrible danger I was in. They laughed and talked me down and I ran off, finally feeling safe until I thought I had caught rabies patting the kitten next door.

During the day we'd read books, play cards and have as much fun as you could at the beach when it was ten degrees outside and you were wearing a rolled-neck jumper. One of our favourite pastimes was scouring the ground for tangles of fishing line and cutting them apart to grab the hooks, swivels and sinkers. Sometimes we'd find an old cork handline and we'd assemble all our stuff in a box, and then never actually go fishing.

On our last morning at The Shack nobody was sad about leaving. We took the dog for one last run down the beach to make the most of what we weren't going to miss. The normally clear sand was covered in half-metre-high mounds of seaweed. We decided to use them as giant trampolines and as soon as we got up in the air we saw a thin white paper nautilus shell lying amongst the seaweed. My brother picked it up and I spied another. For the next half hour we combed the mounds and collected a dozen of these beautiful things, taking them back to the car to show Mum and Dad.

When we got home Mum put a couple in the bathroom, another on her windowsill and the rest in a cupboard. Over the years as they were dropped, hit by a footy or a wayward tennis ball their place was taken by another from the stash in the cupboard. Today there is just the one remaining, and it lives in Mum's bathroom.

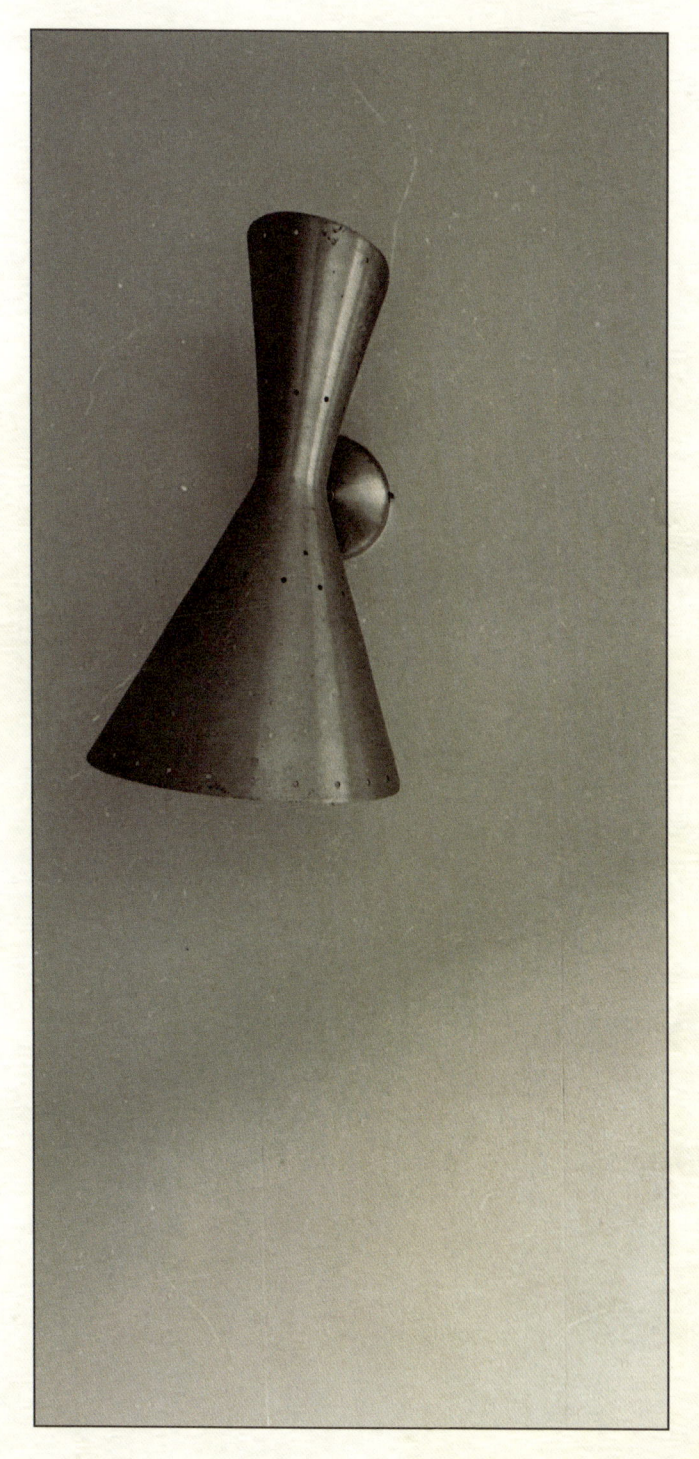

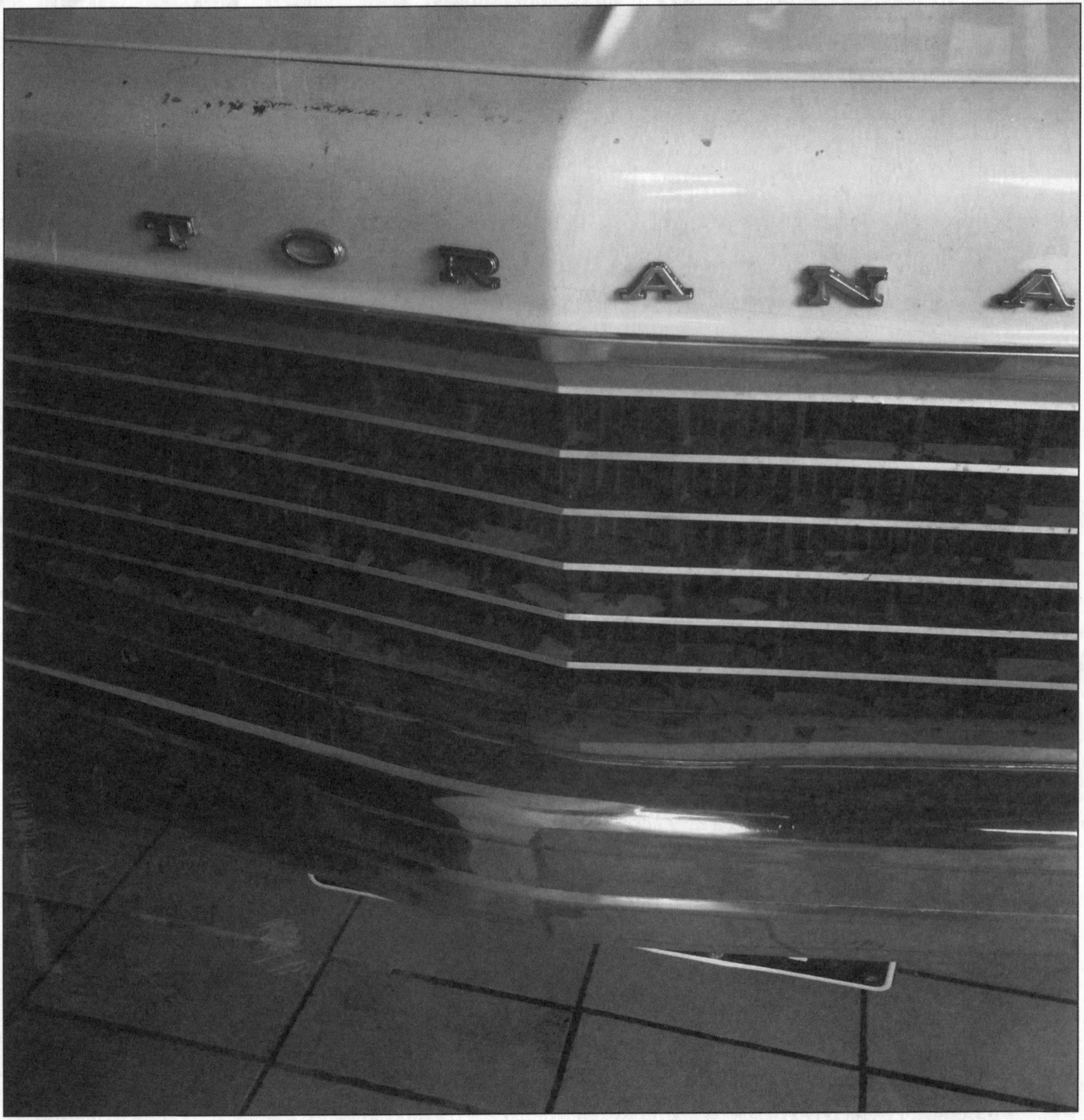
TORANA

CHAPTER 5

The First McMansion on the Block

In his book *The Australian Ugliness*, Australian architect Robin Boyd rallied against Featurism in houses. In 1986, my mate Graham's family built a new house that not only embraced Featurism but grew it a new set of tits.

They'd bought a slightly run-down 1950s beach house, bulldozed immediately and built themselves what could possibly be a two hundred-year reminder of the excesses of the eighties. It was a three-story salmon-rendered brick palace with a faux tower that gave our suburb a well-needed injection of Disneyland Glamour. Instead of a moat they built a matching salmon-rendered wall around the house to keep them safe from having any connection with the beach that was only a hundred metres away. The house had a one-stop lift that took you straight from the six-car garage upstairs to reveal about as much marble that you could throw at an interior.

The house sat on the bottom of the hill and overlooked a yacht club that was built in the early 1960s. To become a member of the club you needed to be nominated by an existing member. Then the committee would post your name on the notice board in the New Members column and if after two weeks nobody had put a drawing pin into your name, you were accepted. The members also had a social tennis club where on Saturday afternoons they took it in turns to host games in their homes. Graham's parents were members and from what I saw it had very little to do with tennis and everything to do with infidelity. Whenever couples arrived and greeted, hands landed and lingered on tennis-skirted bottoms and kisses on cheeks slid to lips. "Let me show you where the bathroom is Pam" was code for 'It's time for me to see your caesar scar'.

Graham and I played footy together and when I first met him he lived in a modest but very well-maintained weatherboard house opposite the footy ground. Finding out what your mate's Dad did for a living in the 1980s was never straightforward. Graham knew his Dad had an office because that's where he drove his Porsche to every day. He also knew that whatever he did had something to do with Smurfs toys. He didn't say it but for a time I suspected he may have actually thought his Dad was Papa Smurf. What he did know was that one day his Mum went from driving a Gemini to driving a Range Rover and they suddenly had loads of money.

It was a common story at the time. Friends were getting pools put in and their folks bought apartments on the Gold Coast. The Dads swapped old tight tees for pink polos and seemed to perpetually have Crown Lager froth on their moustaches. Unfortunately, amongst all this action, the 1980s fairy forgot to visit our house.

Graham and his sister both had an ensuite and a colour TV in their rooms. They also had a separate family TV room, which had sliding doors that opened on to the massive pool. Whenever I went over I was more than happy to indulge in some school holiday resort-style living. If we weren't in the pool or helping ourselves to his massive fridge, we were lying on one of the grey leather lounges watching videos.

Graham's Mum never seemed comfortable in the house and was constantly ordering home-delivered pizzas because she was scared of using the kitchen in case she got it dirty. She was a tiny woman, a bit over five foot, and she struggled to pull herself into the driver's seat of the Range Rover and had to sit on a cushion to see over the steering wheel. She was always welcoming and happy for us to stay over, and actually seemed embarrassed by the size of the house and how soulless it felt without people in it.

One day Graham's Dad came home from the Smurf factory with a CD player. Graham was obsessed and his favourite phrase became "You haven't heard Dire Straits until you've heard them on compact disc". The accuracy of this statement can still be debated but what couldn't was that he was porking up from the home-delivered pizzas. Not that his extra weight stopped him from having a series of cute girlfriends. He was always a friendly and confident guy, but the mega-pad suddenly gave him an edge with the girls from the local private ladies college. His parents were very social and went out most Friday nights, which left him alone in the house. His standard modus operandi was to a invite girl over to watch *Ghost* and share some pepperoni pizza. By the end of the night he always managed to score himself a rushed handjob and was going steady.

Graham wasn't scared of helping himself to the booze in his Dad's substantial cellar under the house. He'd worked out that the safest ploy was to sneak bottles that his Dad had the most of, which seemed logical. That meant we usually ate our Hawaiian pizza with a bottle of 1982 Grange.

Graham had his sixteenth birthday coming up and managed to talk his parents into letting him have a party at their house. Thankfully we had just come though the last days of roller skating; a few short years earlier and the party would have been at Roller City and everyone besides me would have been eagerly waiting for the speedskate sign to illuminate. I hated roller skating. Despite using every free Roller City voucher that I got in a Cadbury showbag, I could never master it. I would clomp rather than skate around the rink and spend most of my time clinging to the carpet walls or lying on the floor. When I was ten, I worried about how I'd cope in the future when I had a girlfriend and wouldn't be able to couple skate, a romantic tradition when lovers in matching tight stretch blue jeans would hold hands and skate around the rink to 'Hopelessly Devoted To You' from the *Grease* soundtrack. The other thing that disturbed me at Roller City were the men in their forties who had been inspired by Cliff Richards in the 'Wired For Sound' film clip. On Saturday afternoons these creepy men with bum-parted blow-dried hair would hoist their easy-fit pleated jeans up to the waist so their arse had something to eat and skate for hours. They only stopped to buy themselves a Choc Wedge or feign an injury so they could lie on the ground and upskirt a teenage girl.

A bunch of us had organised to meet in the park before Graham's party and pre-load with a charming cocktail of warm UDLs and Island Coolers. I was sporting a blonde mullet and wore a grey Jag shirt buttoned to the collar, baggy black jeans and pointy black suede shoes, topped with a World War 2 German army greatcoat. I looked like I was doing Year 10 work experience as a synth player in a New Wave band.

I'd heard that Kristy, one of the girls coming to the party, liked me. I liked her too, mostly because I'd heard she liked me. Kristy had been going out with a boy in the year above us but he'd gone to Canada as an exchange student and after a series of heartfelt letters they had decided to break up. I worked out that the best way to make a move was by being scared to talk to her and avoiding her at all costs. At one stage I almost said hi while 'Blister in the Sun' by The Violent Femmes played for the tenth time, but I walked the other way at the last moment.

Most teenage parties involved one of the girls being upset about something inane and then the girls would take her off to comfort her. Then one of the boys would work out that 'comforting means' touching so they quickly joined the therapy session and with all things going to plan, ended up sucking face with sad girl who could no longer remember why she was upset in the first place.

Before this could happen, we were interrupted by some bogans who turned up in a Torana to crash the party. A few months before just around the corner, a sixteen year old girl had called an open house party when her folks had gone away for the weekend. Things weren't particularly pretty when a bunch of guys turned up in cars and started throwing pot plants against the wall and chucking garden furniture in the pool. By the time the police arrived the party had scattered, windows were broken, the carpet was ruined and her Dad's ride-on mower was sitting in the bottom of the pool.

Expecting trouble, Graham's Dad was prepared. He was sitting on the balcony enjoying what was left of his Grange when he saw the Torana coming round the corner. He calmly closed the electric gates and picked up the garden hose. When the first one got out of the front passenger side wearing a beanie, a footy jumper and a pair of moccasins he pulled the trigger on the pistol nozzle and hosed him like a dog on a hot day. Shocked and furious he retreated into the car. One by one and on multiple occasions they tried to get out of the car and each time he saturated both them and the inside of the vehicle. They were trapped; their only options were to ram the gate or go home and get a towel. As they left they wound down the windows and screamed, "Fuck off you rich poofters!".

The hosing of the bogans had changed the vibe of the party and Graham's Dad was an instant hero. It also gave me a reason to talk to Kristy. She was more casual than the other girls, dressed in black Doc Martens, black tights, a short cord skirt and — the staple of the time — a black long-sleeve Cherry Lane top with a pocket on the front. She was confident and outgoing, which made her both attractive and intimidating. She had long brown hair with a straight fringe and a small constellation of light freckles that spread across her face. Apparently she had seen me get off the bus after school and that seemed to be enough to pique her interest. Her Dad was a local real estate agent and his office was right next to the bus stop so she most spent most days there after school. The local footy club had been sponsored by her Dad for a while but after the senior coach made a crack about him wearing white slip-on shoes to an after-game function, he pulled the pin on the sponsorship and punched out the coach.

After talking for a while I suggested we head down to the beach and we snuck out the side gate and down the uneven steps through the tea trees to the sand. When we got there we sat down and I produced another warm can of vodka and orange out of my greatcoat pocket. We took turns having sips of the sickly sweet liquid, and on her third sip she put her head back and finished the rest of the can.

Next came a mixture of lips, tongues and teeth hitting braces as we pashed in that awkwardly frantic way that only teenagers can. Hands just started going places that were interesting when she pulled away from me, took a deep breath and projectile vomited all over me. Not surprisingly, at sixteen this wasn't a deal-breaker, and after scraping what mess I could off my jacket with a stick, I was happy to resume activities. Suddenly there was a torch. Graham's Dad had sprung us. He called me a bloody idiot and told us to go back to the house,

40

giving me a gentle kick in the arse as I went up the hill. Given that I was covered in spew, I would have preferred him to spray me with the hose.

After our interaction on the beach it was determined that Kristy and I were officially 'going out'. Going to her house was a strange experience because her bedroom was basically in the kitchen. She was the youngest of four girls and used to share a room with her youngest sister but they didn't get on. She demanded a room of her own from her parents but as they didn't have one spare, they took the table out of the kitchen area, replaced it with her bed, knocked up a curtain and suddenly she had her own room where she could also smell the toast burning. The kitchen had pine cupboards and a cork floor so she had the fine distinction of having her very own colonial-style bedroom. The good thing about this arrangement was that there was never any issue about us not being allowed to go into her room; if we were getting a snack we couldn't avoid it.

When I was there, though, I didn't get to spend much time with her. As soon as I walked in the door, her Dad acted exactly like a guy with four daughters, and couldn't get me on the couch watching the cricket quick enough. We'd sit there talking sport and he'd give me a beer or two and Kristy would either sulk, crack the shits or both.

Having only daughters was tough for her Dad and he was still shaken from when they got a new puppy and it came bolting out of his oldest daughter's room with a large black dildo in its mouth. The pup was too fast for the girls so it was up to him to wrestle it out of the dog's jaws. After a laboured tussle, he threw the mangled thing in the bin and went for a very long drive.

When the summer holidays were in full swing Kristy and I went to the beach every day with friends. While the girls read *Dolly* magazines, gossiped and smoked menthol cigarettes, we skimmed a tennis ball off the bay and took it for granted that we could see them in their bikinis. I hated taking my t-shirt off at the beach because I was embarrassed that I didn't have any underarm hair. When I did have to take it off to go for a swim or get a tan, I'd try not to raise my arms. As a result, when I tried to throw a frisbee I looked like a short teenage Peter Garrett dancing in a blonde mullet wig.

Mine and Kristy's romance was interrupted when she headed off to the Gold Coast for a two-week holiday and family reunion. Before she left, we sat on her bed and whispered "I love you" to each other while her Mum made a casserole less than a metre away. I missed her like crazy, could barely eat and waited for the postman out the front every day hoping for a letter. When one did arrive, she'd written pages about how she was missing me and how bored she was and the only thing that was okay was hanging out with her eighteen year old cousin who had come over from London for the reunion. I wrote her a sappy pile of words in return and kept her letter in the top drawer of my bedside table. The next week went slowly. We had a heat wave and my brothers and I lay on our scratchy brown modular lounge like seals on a rock and watched the cricket. Another letter never came but she called me as soon as she got home and we arranged to meet at the beach the next morning. I rode my racer down the bay road and found her sitting against one of the boat sheds. Her tan had deepened and she seemed older. We kissed for a while and then she stopped suddenly.

"I've got something to tell you".

She went on to say how boring the weeks had been without me and how her cousin from London was such a nice guy and how he played in a band and was super cool. She told me how they'd been to Movie World and got on so well because they had so much in common. They had become good friends and then sometime in the second week they went down to the beach at night and started kissing, and then they had sex on the sand, then in the house, and pretty much anywhere they could think of where their grandmother wouldn't catch them.

It was one thing to compete with an older boy from London who played in a band, but it was a different shade of tricky to try and compete with a member of her own family. I was shocked, angry and holding back tears. I told her it was over, raced up the hill and threw my bike against a bin. It did nothing to the bike or the bin. I was heartbroken for the best part of a week. Things were also bad for Graham's Dad. He came home from the Smurf factory one day to find the bogans had spray-painted 'Poofter Pink Palace' on his front wall.

CHAPTER 6

The Birth

It was four o'clock on a winter afternoon in June and we were standing in the kitchen when I started one of those ridiculous conversations with my pregnant wife that never end well. It was along the lines of, "Why do you always buy cabbage? You never cook it and you don't really like it, but you always buy it." I thought it was a reasonable question. People buying food that they didn't like or never ate shat me ever since an old housemate used to buy apricot Yoplait yoghurt for himself out of our sharehouse kitty and then never touch the stuff. As soon as I opened my mouth I realised that I was looking for logic in all the wrong places. There wasn't going to be an outcome that was going to make either party start doing cartwheels and I should have known better, going from past domestic discussions.

One time, I was getting ready to attend a function. It was one of those events where a gaggle of women spent the afternoon getting spray tans and having their beavers ransacked by the same Eastern suburbs beautician, an unlikely millionaire who was as skilled in extracting information as she was at removing pubic hair. In a magnificent self-feeding frenzy, she would pry a deep, dark secret

44

from one woman then pass it on to the next, so not only did she have a constant flow of chit-chat but also ensured that the event would be buzzing with scurrilous gossip. I always dreaded greeting these ladies in their ridiculously towering high heels because their faces would fight their Botox when my beard met their cheek for a kiss. You could feel them recoil and then strain out a grimace, like they were producing an uncooperative turd, at the thought of my beard removing half of their two hundred dollar makeup job.

Running late for the function with the cab beeping in the driveway, I was trying to press a shirt but couldn't find the iron anywhere. Pivoting in my undies with the Fabulon in hands I picked up my phone.

"Baby, do you know where the iron is by any chance?"

A little pause as I heard her replying to a work email.

"In the cupboard where the potatoes used to be."

"Oh for fuck's sake," I muttered as I wasted valuable time considering the next question.

"So where do the potatoes live now? In the laundry?"

"In the pantry next to the Rodney Dangerfield glasses."

It was a done deal. The potatoes no longer lived in the custom-made vegetable drawer, but had instead taken up personal residence next to a set of tumblers that I picked up at a Venice Beach garage sale, which had supposedly come from the estate of the late, great American comedian Rodney Dangerfield. How could anyone resist a set of six for eight bucks? Not I, and they are still a conversation starter all these years later.

Now, as the cabbage conversation reached that point where I truly regretted bringing it up we both noticed a puddle of water on the floor. Normally I would have blamed the fridge, but it definitely wasn't the fridge leaking, it was my wife, and we both had the realisation that:
A. Our first baby was on the way; and
B. I was probably going to be the one who had to get the paper towel out to clean the baby juice off the floor.

I was excited about becoming a father but incredibly ambivalent about baby books and birthing classes. Michelle had got the lot and studied them intently at night while I preferred to get slightly drunk. I'd had a glance at one called *Are You Ready To Give Up Everything?* Or maybe it was *I've Made A Fortune On Preying On Your Fear Of Giving Birth*. It had a list of things that pregnant mothers shouldn't eat. Amongst the standard things like salami, soft cheeses and smacky ecstasy, it also listed bananas. According to this book, bananas are responsible for giving expectant Mummies a congested vagina. I don't know what a congested vagina is but I'm sure it can't be cured with a pack of Butter Menthols.

I had also been dragged to a full weekend course on how to give birth without the use of the finest chemicals invented by man. On this two-day bore fest we sat around in IKEA chairs, watched videos, drew pictures of what we thought the baby would look like and massaged our wives in front of complete strangers. The course was taken by a woman with the posture of a preying mantis, who revelled in wearing happy pants and I'm sure could make a visit to Aldi look like a yoga class. The first thing she said at the start of the class was, "Did anyone else have a hard time with the traffic from Bondi?" I was sure she was going to follow it up with, "Has anyone tried to get Pete Evans to give you a kale enema?" At the pub for lunch after the first session on day one, I casually suggested to Michelle that we leave and not come back. She disagreed and I had another schooner. After two days of this torture I had the following revelations: my wife was serious about having the baby sans opiates, and if I really wanted to sit on an IKEA chair with a bunch of strangers, next time I'd just go to IKEA.

Amongst the sea of information about the birth, I had remembered where the hospital was and where to park. Once I had put Michelle into the car with the delivery bag that had been sitting next to the door for a month, we were at the hospital in no time. Michelle didn't seem to think she was having contractions; all we knew for sure was that her waters had broken. I parked the car out the front in the loading zone. The midwife on our pre-birth tour had stressed that we could park in the loading zone for as long as we wanted and to not stress out about it. This was music to my ears. I had once driven my old 1963 EH Holden to the SCG with the intention of not drinking, unaware that our tickets were in a catered box with full bar service. Good intentions went out the window. I cabbed it home and it took me two days to get around to picking up my car. When I left, it was one of hundreds parked on the grass opposite the stadium. When I returned, it sat alone in the middle of the park like some sort of Sculpture By The Sea installation.

For some reason private hospitals are often painted Tuscan yellow to resemble an early-nineties Italian restaurant. It's quite confusing because you don't know whether someone is going to take out a cancerous growth or make you an overpriced seafood risotto. Michelle waddled in while I grabbed the bag and locked the car, safe in the knowledge that it could be sitting in that loading zone for a week.

One of the interesting choices you have when you find out you are having a baby is that you can either buy yourself a second-hand Corolla, or give that same money to an obstetrician. We decided to give the Toyota the miss and gamble the coin on someone who had spent the same amount of time to do two degrees as I did to get my singular Arts degree. Of course, one of the benefits of having an obstetrician is that the pregnant woman builds a rapport with them over the months as the baby grows so by the time it's D-Day you're practically besties when the sheets are covered in after-birth and they are reaching for the needle and thread.

Finding the right one proved initially difficult because Michelle was relying on the insane chatter of complete strangers on internet baby forums. It seemed that people like Mrs Wikibabyleaks of Chatswood was happy to accuse anyone who had ever donned a white coat for malpractice except for Dr Kildare (probably because she hadn't heard of this 1960s TV doctor played by Richard Chamberlain). In the end we took a massive risk and took the old-fashioned approach of asking our GP for a recommendation. I know it seems crazy to seek the opinion of someone who is qualified but this was a chance I was prepared to take. So with the help of our GP we chose a rather happy physician named Dr Stan who had a fantastic sense of humor, gave us his mobile phone number (a rarity for any specialist) and was prone to wearing his slacks so high that they almost rubbed on his bosoms. Predictably I dubbed him Dr Stan the High-Pants Man. I happily went along to most of the pre-natal visits, partly because I wanted to be involved, but mostly because I wanted to see where the money went. He had a modest office and his waiting room was always filled with a mixture of women who were pregnant for the first time and generally slightly nervous but happy, and women who were on to baby number two or three, with no nerves at all and miserable because they were too large and slow to stop their toddlers from putting a *Women's Weekly* in the fish tank.

Once we had put down the credit card for the room we went straight up to the birthing suite and this is when we hit our first major hurdle. The midwife put Michelle on the bed, placed a heart monitor on the bub and asked us who our obstetrician was. When I replied "Dr Stan the High-Pants Man" nobody laughed. The midwife disappeared for a moment and then returned.

"I'm sorry but Dr. Stan is away fishing this weekend and isn't available but we have a very good locum who is going to look after you."

I'd like to pretend that the first thing that came out of my mouth was "That seems very fair and reasonable; I'm looking forward to meeting a complete stranger who is about to spend some quality time with my wife's vagina", but I'm afraid I would be lying. We were shitty, but knew it wasn't uncommon for overpaid medicos to head off to their beach houses in Noosa at the drop of a speculum and leave you high and dry.

When my Mum was a practising General Practitioner she did a lot of obstetrics. Still to this day, when I'm in the supermarket with her she bumps into ex-patients whose babies she delivered, and then those babies grew up into pregnant mums, whose babies she also delivered. As a kid the home phone would constantly ring in the middle of the night and she'd jump up and get in the car, head to the hospital, deliver a baby and be back in time to watch me try and lodge a spoon in my brother's skull over breakfast.

In the mid-eighties I'd been inspired by those American teen movies where the characters had phones in their bedrooms. I found an old phone in a cupboard and removed the bells so it wouldn't ring and then went searching under the house for the phone line, which fortunately ran right under my room. I made a junction of the wires with the aid of a Stanley knife and some electrical tape, drilled a hole through my bedroom floor, poked the line up and wired it into a socket. Before I knew it, and without my folks having any inkling, I was sitting on my bed talking to my mates like Molly Ringwald* in *Sixteen Candles*. I kept the phone hidden under my bed and one night I must have knocked it off the hook by accident and the hospital couldn't get through to Mum to ask her to come in and deliver a baby. Was Mum angry when she found out about my new phone? Yes. Was Dr Stan the High-Pants Man not being there for the birth of my first son karma for the phone incident? Once my wife reads this, the answer will also be Yes.

I'll be honest and say that I've never really been a subscriber to getting involved in the technical side of having a baby. I am aware of the concept of things like counting contractions but don't have my head fully around that side of the game. My overarching view of the birthing process is to leave it in the hands of those who have a tertiary education specialising in such things. Not that I'm saying that I couldn't deliver the baby of a stranger on public transport; in fact I'd be Johnny On The Spot calling for hot towels and someone to Google how to cut an umbilical cord with your teeth. In the field, when the pressure is on and you are the only hope for the future, like Obi-Wan Kenobi, you step up; but in a hospital, I say sit back and watch the magicians at work. It is my view that if you have people in the room who do it every day for a living, let them do their thing.

I saw it as my job to take Michelle's mind off things by asking inane questions. When we were moved into the delivery suite it seemed quite normal to question the utilitarian yet floral chairs in the room. What expectant mother doesn't want to

*For the young people reading, imagine if the Kardashians had an adopted freckly, ginger sister who wasn't a dick and you'll get an idea of how big Molly was in the 1980s.

hear an impromptu speech on the folly of badly designed hospital furniture?

For some reason, while Michelle was on the hospital bed phone to her Mum I decided to download a game to my phone. I don't really like games; I've never really played them but something in me snapped — let's call it nervous energy. I was suddenly playing some obscure Angry Birds-type mission where I had to blow things up with hand grenades. Michelle thought I was downloading an app to measure contractions and I thought for the sake of the baby it was best to play along and while she thought I figuring out how to make it work I was actually blowing up castles on Level 4 and had just scored a rocket launcher.

There wasn't much going on, even according to the birth plan that we put together with the help of the baby class instructor who was now writing a book called something like *How To Quit Being Interesting*. Birthing plans are best known for being ripped up as soon as the going gets tough but they often look like this:

- I would like our baby to come into the world drug-free.
- I would like to play our own music in the birthing suite.
- I would like to use scented oils to relieve pressures and pain during the birth of our child.
- I would only like to be offered drugs at the last possible moment, when there isn't anyone left in a ten kilometre radius who I haven't called a fucking arsehole.
- I would like to use candles in the room to create atmosphere.

These baby classes always recommend having a birthing plan, which suggest burning candles to relax the mother while in labour. Despite being supposed experts in the field, they haven't seemed to realise there is not a hospital in Australia where you can light a candle because every hospital bed has oxygen coming out of a tap, so if it came into contact with the open flame of an over-priced scented candle it would blow the hospital back to way before Gough introduced universal health care.

Michelle was starting to get slightly tetchy as things that I will never understand started happening to her body. I took a quick break from Grenade Force to put on the playlist I had put together. It had a bunch of mellow songs inspired by a Sigur Ros album that we listened to at night. Sigur Ros are a band from Iceland who make beautiful atmospheric music that most people probably listen to while taking drugs, rather than avoid taking drugs like Michelle was hoping to do. Unfortunately after two to three songs Michelle told me that she "fucking hated that music" in a slightly ungentle way. I deduced that the pain was getting worse as she panted and took deeper breaths and gave me subtle hints to how she was feeling, like "shit this hurts."

The nurse came in to see how things were going and suggested an Icy Pole might help. I agreed; it had been ages since I'd had an Icy Pole and was feeling rather parched. It was only when she came back with one that I realised it was for Michelle and not me. It seemed to work a bit and Michelle asked me to go get her another one. I agreed, thinking I could also get one for myself. But as soon as I asked at the nursing station I realised they had cottoned on to me, because the midwife said that she'd bring one in shortly and when she did, she made a point of unwrapping it and putting it straight into Michelle's hand and didn't leave until she was sure that Michelle was going to eat it.

As the hours progressed, the pain increased and then stopped and I passed the time by making Michelle green tea that she didn't drink and trying to get through Level 12 on my game. We had been waiting to see the locum and when he finally came into the room he apologised profusely for not getting in earlier as he'd been delivering another baby. I believed him because I'd heard the screams when I was down the corridor helping myself to my fourth Scotch Finger biscuit from the kitchenette.

Rick, as he introduced himself, was a really nice guy and made Michelle feel at ease straight away. A tall ginger bloke with a warm smile, he looked so familiar but I couldn't put my finger on where I knew him from. As soon as he walked out the door I worked it out.

"He's Dr Rick from the *Today* show!"

Michelle had no idea what I was talking about.

"He's the expert on the *Today* show on Channel Nine... This is almost like Karl Stefanovic delivering our baby!"

I was impressed but she still wasn't interested and sent me off to get another Icy Pole.

By this stage her mum had arrived and this gave me a chance to get to the next level on my game and then get a bit of rest on the fold-out couch. It was nice to have Michelle's mum take over for a while, as I'd been trying out every different pressure spot and massage technique I'd learnt at the stupid birthing classes and each effort was rewarded with differing versions of "Please don't touch me."

It seemed nothing much was really happening but it proved to be the calm before the storm. Before I could get to the next level I was standing by uselessly as Michelle moved into every position available to try and ease the pain. She was doing well but as time went on the pain got too much and she called for the epidural. It was a Friday night and as the anaesthetist wasn't sitting around playing canasta in the staff room, they had to cal him in from home to administer it. I once worked with a guy who refused to let his wife have one despite her pleas during labour because he thought they were a rip-off. I've been married for a little while now and I know in the long run, pulling out the Visa would be far easier than copping grief for the next fifty years. It must have been four minutes after she'd asked for the epidural that she started demanding I find out when it was going to happen. I managed to stall her a few minutes before I had to go down to the nurse station to ask how long it would be. When I returned Michelle was standing up, bracing for her next contraction. I managed to relay that the anaesthetist was on his way from his house just as she copped a belt of pain.

"Find out what fucking suburb he's coming from and how long he's going to be!"

I almost caught myself saying that I didn't want to ask, but wisely decided against it. I did a slow lap of the ward, walked back into the room and effortlessly lied.

"Good news, he's coming from Chatswood and he'll be here in ten minutes."

Thankfully he arrived within fifteen, but the first thing he did when he walked in the room was apologise for taking so long to get there from Paddington. I decided to go for another walk around the ward.

When I came back the magic had been done. Michelle was asleep and Dr Rick suggested we all get some rest before the action really kicked in. There wasn't any option other than to share the fold-out bed with my mother-in-law Cheryl. Cheryl is a very social person with the perfect-sized personality. It's large enough to be constantly entertaining but not so large that she's annoying. She does have a worrying addiction to leopard print clothing, which is so advanced she once had the keepers rushing for the tranquiliser guns when she went for a stroll around Dubbo Zoo. When she first met my young friend Stefan the first thing she said was, "Oh my God you look like my first boyfriend Bricey!" Then when she met another of my young mates she said, "Oh my God you look like my first boyfriend Graham." I put a hold on introductions after that.

In circumstances other than the birth of my first child I probably would have slept in the car rather than bed down on a fold-out with my mother-in-law but we were all tired and I needed to reserve my strength to get to Level 17 on the game. Cheryl crashed straight away and I reflected what a slippery slope becoming a grandparent is.

By the time my Nanna became a Nanna, she was a champion at dropping Nanna Farts and never felt the need to apologise. By that stage of her life she either didn't notice or thought they were akin to sneezing. It was an easy routine. Put the stewed apricots in the fridge; drop a Nanna Fart. Waddle into the lounge room to watch the Channel Nine News; not before tooting a few sideways on the journey. It's strange when I think back to that memory of being a child, standing on the Laminex floor in the kitchen next to the concertina sliding door, sun streaming through the kitchen windows, giving some love to the hydrangeas on the way. My grandfather sitting at the kitchen table in his dressing gown and slippers making his way through the crossword in *The Sun*. All of it punctuated by the sound of my maternal grandmother absentmindedly dropping her guts.

The decision whether to stay in the bed or sleep on the floor next to the antibiotic-resistant germs wasn't needed because the screams coming from Michelle's direction told me it was game time. The midwife and Dr Rick were on the scene quicker that you can say "Unfortunately not all of this is covered by your private health insurance."

At this stage, I knew this was where I could get involved and I was ready for action. There's an old joke that watching the baby being born is like watching your favourite pub being burnt down but I'm not a subscriber to that view. Up until that stage the baby was very much an abstract thing. I knew it was in there, I'd seen the scans and watched the tummy grow of course but during that time it was a representative of change rather than something that I could truly picture. My friend Pinko had told me that the baby didn't actually become real for him until it arrived and I certainly felt something similar. It was more like having a present sitting under the Christmas tree for months and knowing that when you open it, it can't be taken back or exchanged.

By now I'd stopped playing the game on the phone and Dr Rick had called me off the bench. He instructed me to grab a leg and he grabbed the other. Michelle was screaming and Dr Rick was calmly telling her when to push. Using our shoulders we had her legs elevated and after three more pushes Dr Rick turned to me.

"What are you up to these days Rosso?"

I had just started to answer him when Michelle interrupted.

"Can you not talk about your job please, I'm trying to deliver our fucking baby!"

It took two hours from there but when our little boy came out everything anyone had ever said about the birth of your child made sense. The surge of emotion, the tears, the love, the pride, the tidal wave of blood — there is not a way to properly describe it. It is the most comprehensively complete positive emotion that you can experience. It's the reason people send gifts of baby clothes. It's got nothing to do with the clothes; there are not too many first-time Mums who haven't got that department covered. It's about sharing a feeling. It's their way of remembering the sheer joy that the birth of their children brought to them.

For the first time in my life time stopped and everything was about Michelle and our beautiful little boy Bugsy. As I gently carried him downstairs in the baby capsule, my mum rang, and on an emotional high I told her I finally understood and appreciated what they had done for me as parents. I suddenly saw my childhood through completely different eyes and I thanked her for the way she'd brought us up and the sacrifices she'd made. After we spent ten minutes making sure Bugsy was secure in the back seat we drove off at twenty kilometres an hour, sans parking ticket.

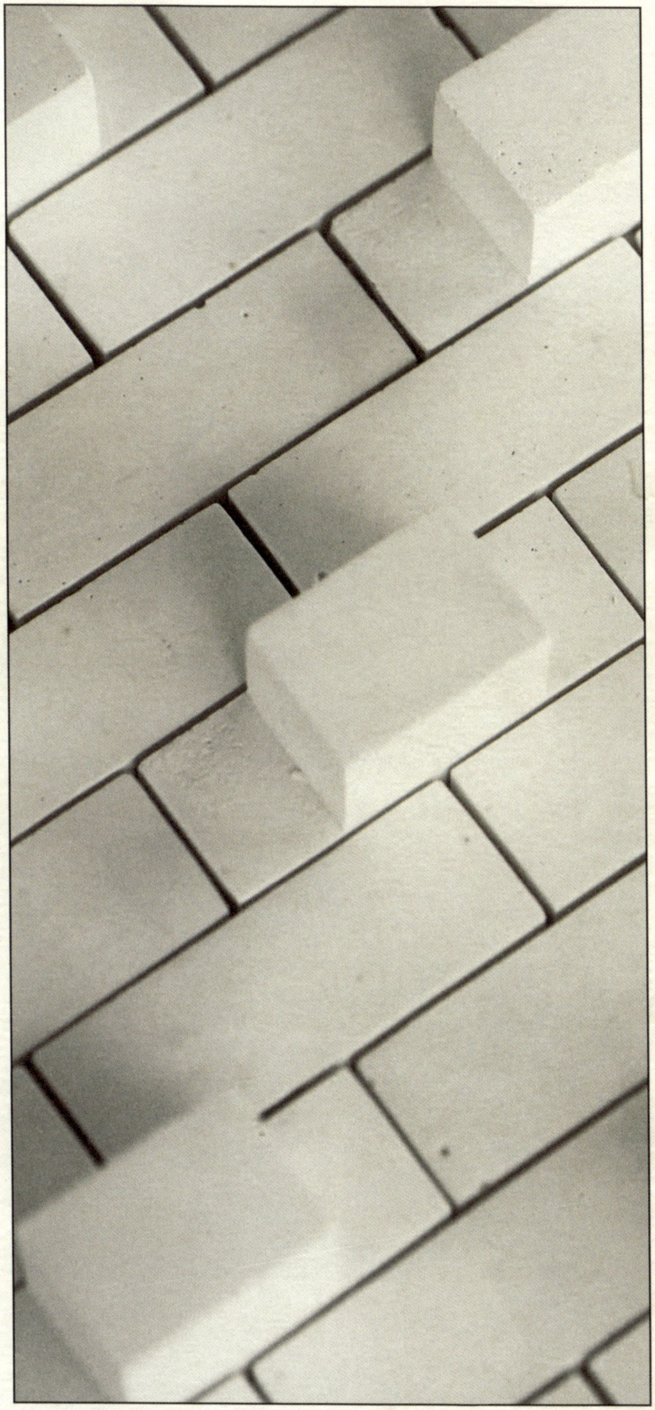

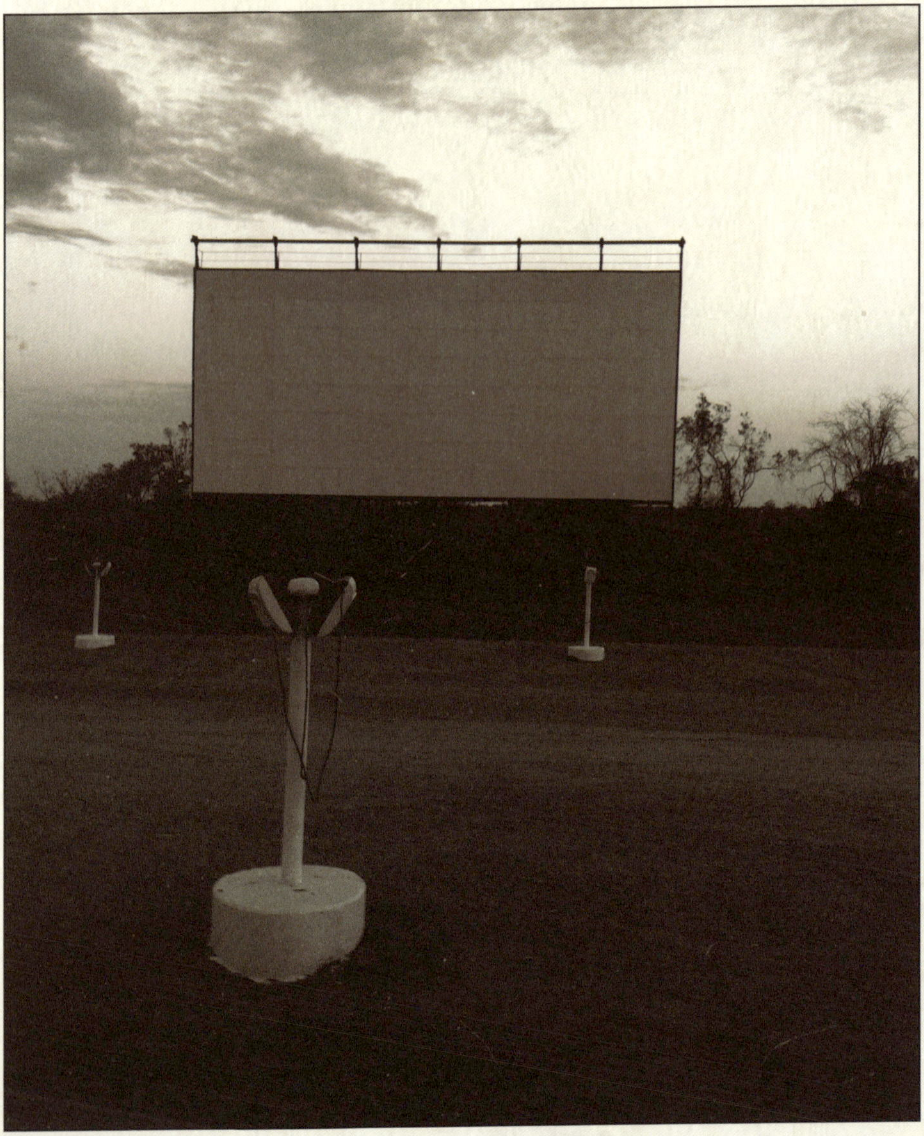

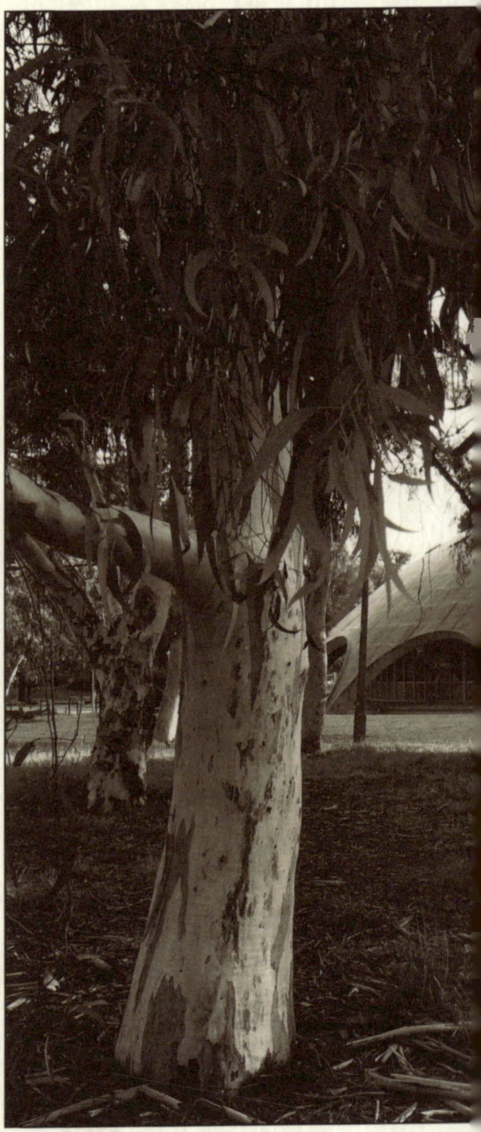

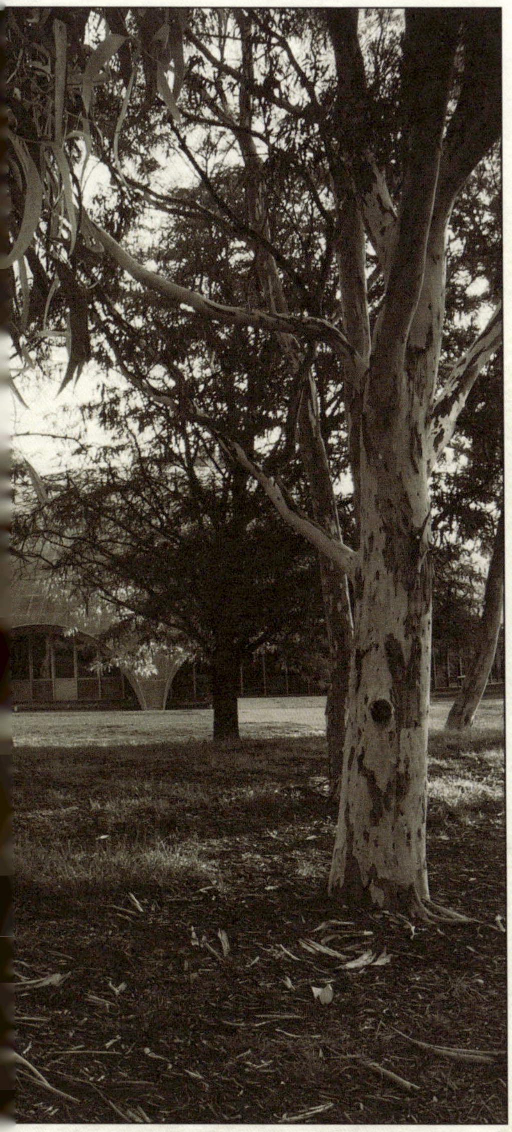
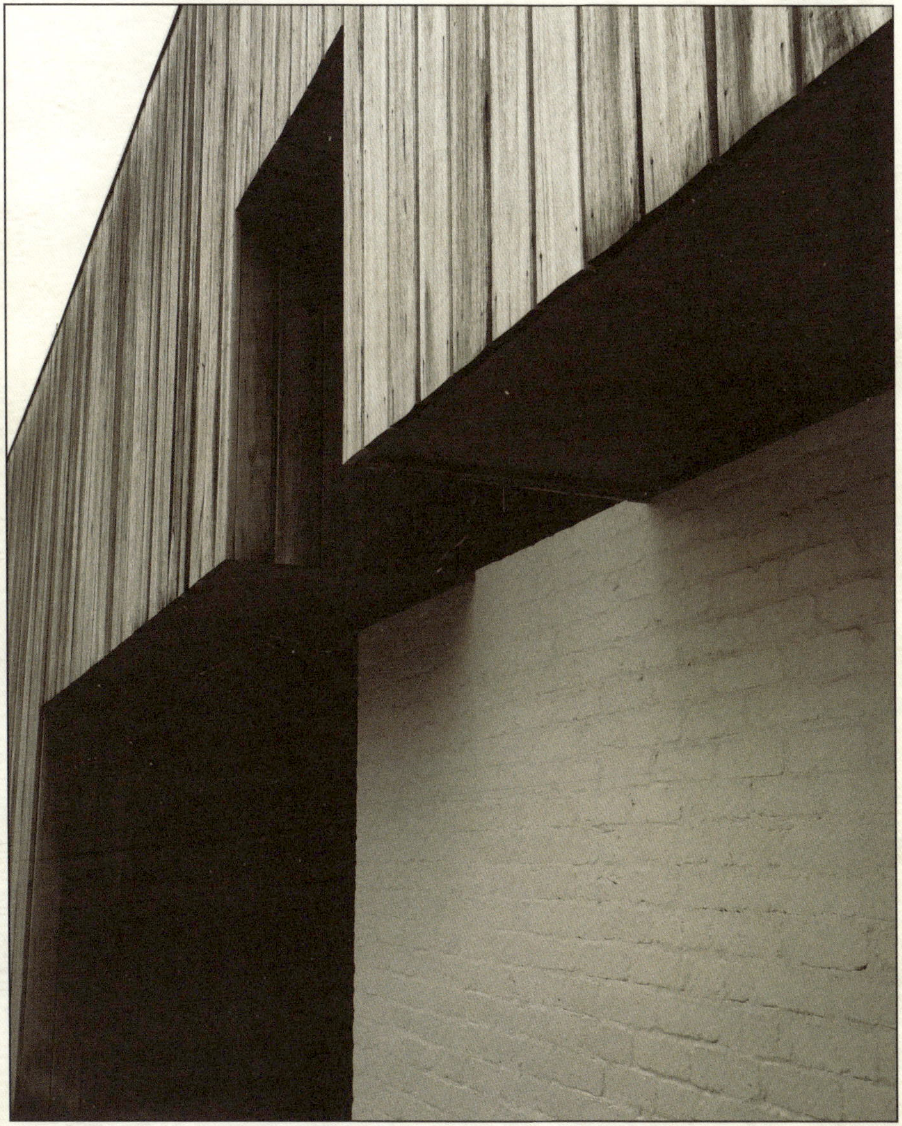

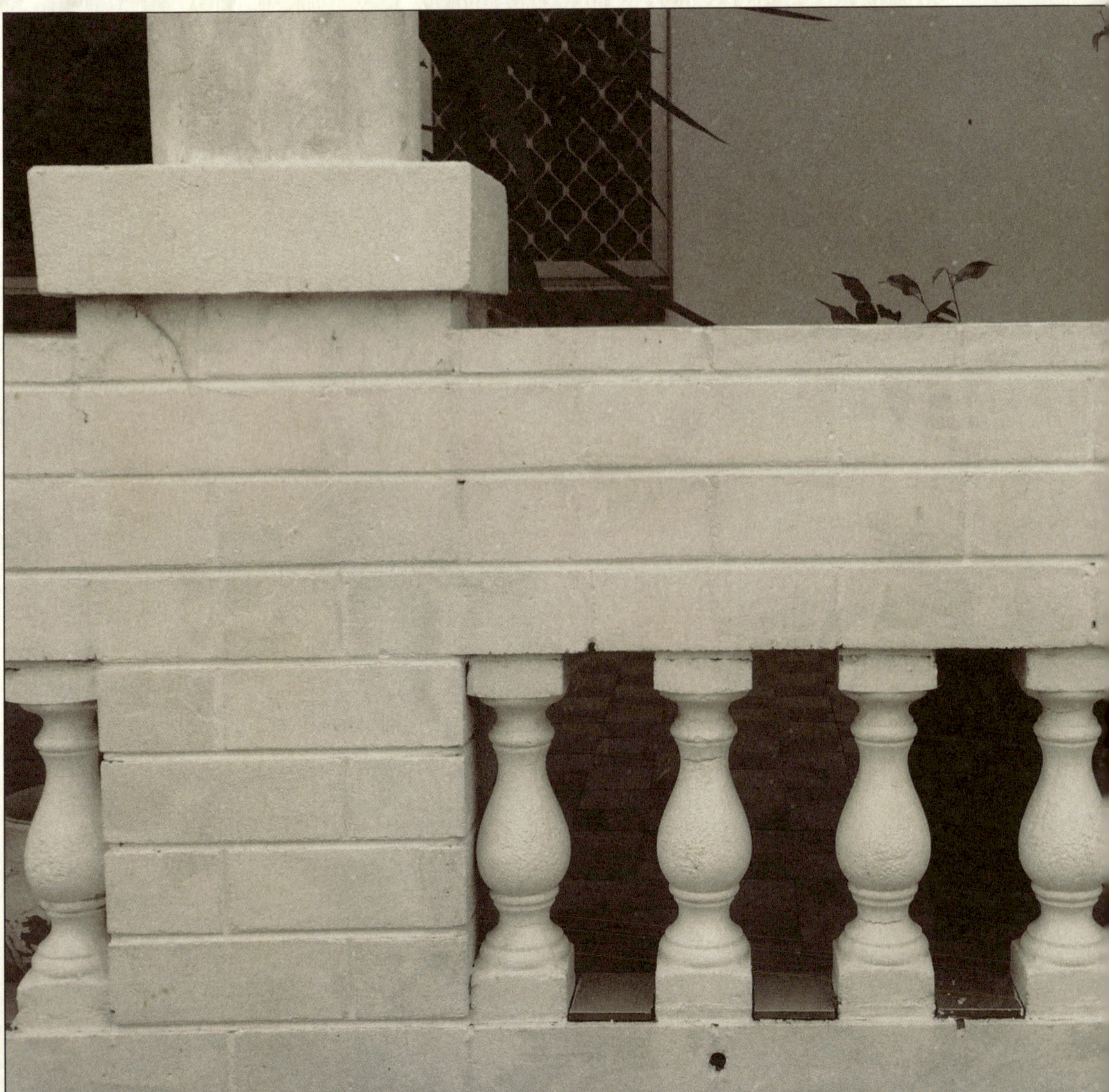

CHAPTER 7

Fremantle Nights

Half-pissed from five hours on the plane, the first thing Dane did was get her to drive him to Fremantle Cemetery to look at Bon Scott's grave.

When he told his Dad he was moving over West his Dad said, "There are only two reasons why a bloke moves to Western Australia — to work in the mines or for a sheila, and both of 'em involve you working your arse off so somebody else can get a diamond."

His Dad would have had a valid point if there were more diamond mines in Western Australia. Also, Dane had spent the last five years working in arts administration and had an inability to work heavy machinery (a mixture of chronic unco-ness and a severe love of alcohol), which left the other reason for moving – love.

He had been seeing her for a year and although she loved Sydney she desperately wanted to move back so she could be close to her family. Her sister had married the world's most boring accountant (hard to believe given the stiff competition for that title), and she wanted to be around to help out with baby wipes.

He didn't have to think long or particularly hard about the move. He knew it was always on the cards so said yes without hesitation. She was so over the moon at his enthusiasm she blew him right then and there on the couch while they were watching the *7.30 Report*. He thought to himself that he should agree to move interstate more often.

Time had only increased the pull, and he couldn't imagine not being around her. This one had worked in every way that the others hadn't. It took him less than a week to find a job online. His new position was at the Fremantle Council coordinating things like drawing classes for old people and hip hop dance competitions for teenagers who liked breaking into cars.

He happily resigned from his current position. For the last three years he'd worked for a festival that had wasted government money trying to get people in Western Sydney to free arty events that they had no interest in or intention in ever attending. Their only reasonable success was an artwork that his boss commissioned from a Christchurch artist that he had the hots for.

His boss may not have got his man but a park in Parramatta did receive *The World's Largest Fried Rice*, a giant sculpture that consisted of a fifteen metre-wide fibreglass wok filled with a mound of plastic fried rice. The crowds had rolled in to see it but only after it had made the front page of the paper when a pair of drug-crazed ice addicts managed to climb into the wok and try to eat the plastic fried rice for tea. Inspired by this success, his boss expanded it into a fully-fledged Sculpture in the Park the following year. The centrepiece was yet another giant sculpture, this time a full-sized illuminated McDonalds Drive Thru sign that was placed in the middle of the park. This sculpture also found its way into the paper when a local geography teacher on the way home from the pub drove his Nissan Patrol seven hundred metres across the park and tried to order himself a McHappy Meal.

She had flown out a week before him, putting her Corolla on the train. He'd toyed with the idea of putting his crappy furniture in his folks' garage, but knew his mum would put it all on Gumtree and order his dad to take whatever she couldn't sell to the tip. She had once put his motorbike on eBay when he went to Bali for a week, so she was definitely capable of it.

He was feeling liberated by the prospect of a fresh start. He didn't bother having farewell drinks and deleted his Facebook account the night before he left. On the flight he felt calm for what felt like the first time in years and celebrated by drinking mini bottles of Shiraz Cabernet and drawing a pair of saggy tits on a picture of Deborah Hutton in the in-flight magazine.

She was easy to spot at the baggage carousel, the only one not wearing hi-vis gear. She wasn't that interested in visiting the grave of the former lead singer of ACDC, was hoping that all he wanted to see was their new home. But it was on the way and would only take a few minutes. She parallel parked the Corolla outside the cemetery and in tandem an old Ford Falcon with sparkling mag wheels and blue metallic paint rumbled in beside them. As they walked down one of the paths for the third time she looked around at row after row of graves and wanted to know how they were supposed to find Bon's. Dane looked at the two lads in the singlets and footy shorts who had jumped out of the Falcon.

"Let's follow the bogans."

They shimmied between the graves, trying not to make it obvious that they were following them. Like a couple of pedestrian ASIO operatives, they meandered behind them for five minutes, occasionally pausing and pretending to look at a headstone. Five minutes turned into ten as they zig-zagged across the cemetery and then around in circles.

She had well and truly had enough.

"Fuck this, I'm going to ask them!"

"No don't, can't we just keep following them?"

"No. We can't."

She skipped twenty metres towards them until she was in earshot.

"Excuse me guys, you don't happen to know where Bon Scott's grave is do you?"

They stopped straight away and looked at each other until one of them sheepishly replied.

"We've got no idea. We thought youse did."

The other joined in.

"Yeah, we've been following youse."

Dane didn't get to see the grave.

This was his first time in Perth and as they drove towards their new home he was shocked by the sheer size of the kangaroo paws growing on the nature strip. The way they reached up and angled slightly towards the road reminded him of Daleks. Everything was the colour of the earth. This was a city where the bush couldn't be defeated, showing its winning hand in the sandy soil, the scorched grass and the bore water-stained gutters in the street he was about to call home.

A series of untamed olive trees partially obscured the house, which was one of her Dad's investment properties. He'd made the most of the 1980s, amazingly avoiding that Perth holy trinity of the time: divorce, jail and heart disease. The only remnants of the era were a series of houses across town, a well-manicured moustache and greying sideburns that made him look like a slightly ruddy George Negus.

Cream brick, the two-storey house had a twin arched carport with mission brown roller doors. A Pebblecrete path led to a Pebblecrete set of stairs and a balcony edged with a balustrade of flaking white columns. A galvanised pipe pergola sat over the driveway covered in grapevines. In small garden beds were an assorted array of cacti; every other surface had been concreted and covered with mustardy brown tiles. She wasn't crazy about the appearance of the house and it's deep Australian-Italian stylings and had a comprehensive list of things to do to improve it. He pretended to listen, just happy to be living rent-free.

It took him all of two days to be completely seduced by the big sky of his adopted city. The lack of daylight savings saw him up at six and jogging around the gentle hills of Freo, down along the water, and saying good morning to strangers before plonking himself down on an outside table at his new favourite café. Every morning he'd drink two, sometimes three, milky lattes and have two slices of thick white toast smothered in margarine and Vegemite. He'd read the paper and watch a group of men finish their bike ride and sit down for breakfast. He soon went from laughing at their lycra-squashed balls to crushing on their Italian racing bikes. He knew it was only a matter of time until he joined them, and without Facebook his old mates would be none the wiser.

Next to the café was a massage place and while waiting for his coffee one morning, the owner Lenny caught him looking at it.

"That place is pretty good. If you go, ask for the special. They'll knock the top off for you."

He tried to wink as he said this but his squat, puffy face turned it into a head-tilting grimace. Dane had actually been staring straight through the building, thinking about the inequality of a New South Welshman being in a work AFL footy-tipping competition. He didn't know what to say to Lenny so he just nodded.

She had quickly put her stamp on the inside of the house and although he jokingly called her eclectic mix of secondhand furniture Shabby Shit, he secretly loved being in the place. They opened up the doors in the afternoon and the breeze would weave though the house and seem to gently lift him up and push him towards the fridge to grab another beer. On the fridge was a list of her favourite baby names under a Margaret River magnet, but he didn't need that to work out that she was clucky. He'd seen her be that woman at a barbecue — the childless one, happy to jump up and down on the trampoline with the kids for hours while their shell-shocked mums hid in the kitchen and manically guzzled Pinot Gris.

Her younger brother had been living in the house before he headed off to Los Angeles to take photos of himself being a douche bag with his shirt off. They had inherited his cleaner, May, a Korean woman in her late thirties who showed little enthusiasm for cleaning products or in fact cleaning full stop. Most of the time she went outside and made phone calls on her mobile while she smoked cigarettes and absentmindedly pulled lemons off the lemon tree. It was decided that she had to go and Dane was nominated for the job of letting her know. He handed her a hundred and thirty-five dollars for her three hours of work.

"I'm sorry May but we're not going to need you next week... and actually we're not going to need you again I'm afraid. You're fired."

Sacking cleaners wasn't his strong point. She counted the money, gave him a death stare and flip-flopped out the door in her pink fluorescent thongs. When the door slammed he yelled out.

"It's done!"

"Good!" she replied from the backyard, while picking up the last of the lemons.

The following Sunday they went for lunch at a pub in Cottesloe for a family birthday. Post-lunch, the girls sat around in the beer garden drinking rosé and passing babies around

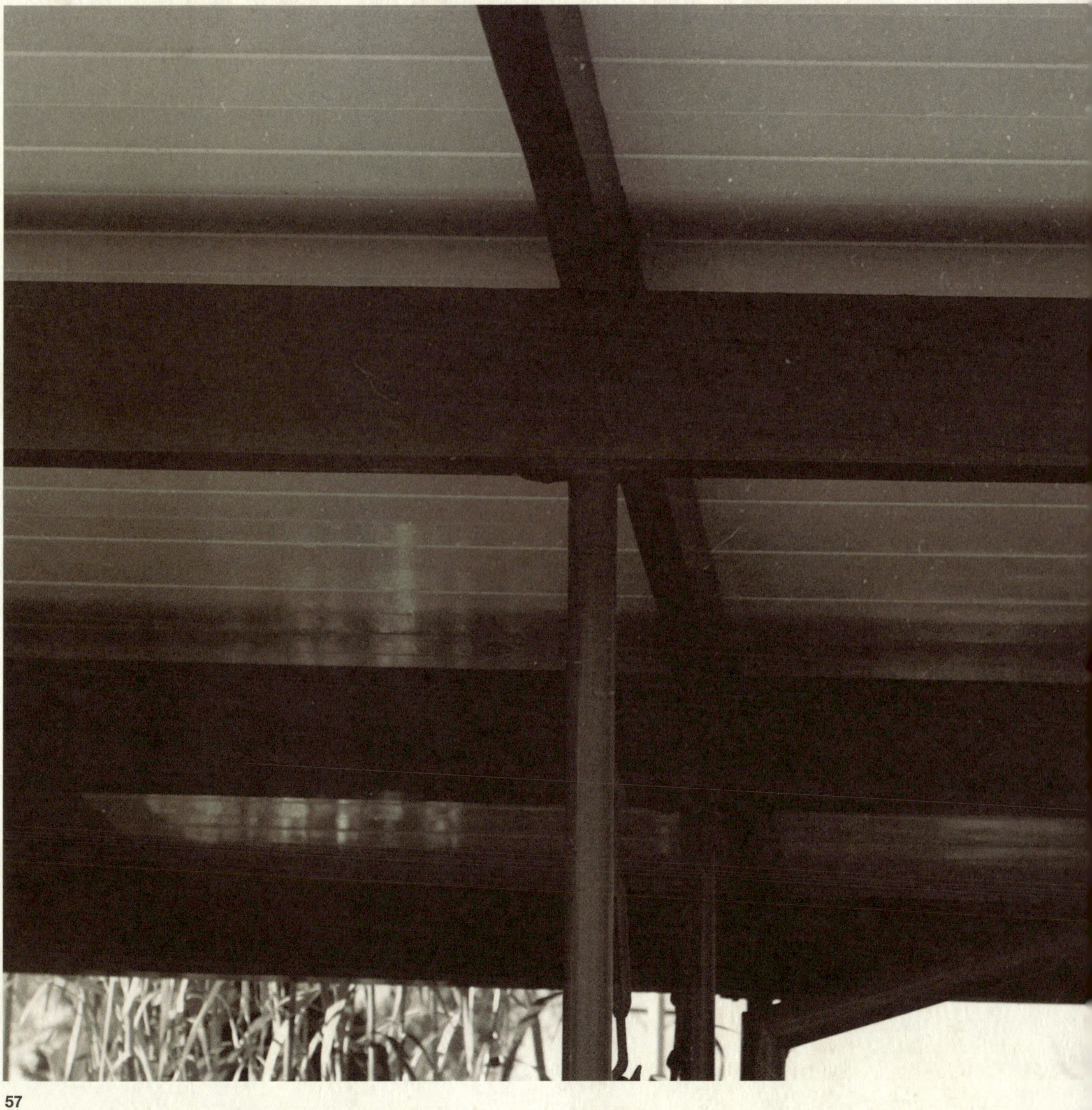

while the boys went to the front bar to drain schooners and have a bet. He wasn't much of a gambler so he just sat at the bar next to an old bloke who looked like a bag full of skin cancers. It was another Sunday afternoon in Perth where everyone drank too much.

She was pissed and happy to be back with her family. They got the cab to drop them off at a little bar in Freo on the way home. As they stood on the footpath out the front she grabbed him.

"Let's have a baby!"

"I think we should wait. I'm not quite ready," he slurred.

What happened next started with "The problem with you is…" and ended with "Why don't you fuck off back to Sydney." Amongst the one-sided tirade was a sledge about his old band and their most successful gig being the support act for Killing Heidi at an underage show.

What wasn't communicated was that he was just scared and that when push came to shove, of course he'd have a baby with her. Also lost was that she didn't really want him to fuck off back to Sydney. It was irrational, wanting to bring a little bundle of school fees into the world with someone and then immediately wanting them to disappear into the land of fourteen dollar street parking.

She stormed off and he happily let her. He walked into the bar, ordered himself a vodka and tonic and started mentally listing all the things he hated about her family. He hadn't got much further than her Mum's pancake arse in a pair of white jeans when he realised how pissed he was. He left the bar and stumbled around the corner, finding himself in front of the massage joint. His drunken mind told him he deserved one for copping such a spray. He walked in past the flashing sign and was hit instantly by the smell of stale air conditioning and catchy Asian pop music.

A bored girl barely looked up from her phone when he walked in.

"Sixty-five dollars, eighty-five if you want special."

"I'll take the special."

"First door on your right. Take your clothes off and lie on the bed. Your masseuse will be with you shortly."

He stumbled as he walked down the hallway and into the room but somehow managed to take his clothes off without falling over. He heaved himself on to the table and lay face-down on a towel that smelt of man sweat. Thirty seconds later the door opened and through the hole in the table he could see a pair of pink fluorescent thongs.

He cranked his neck up.

"Hello Dane!"

It was May.

58

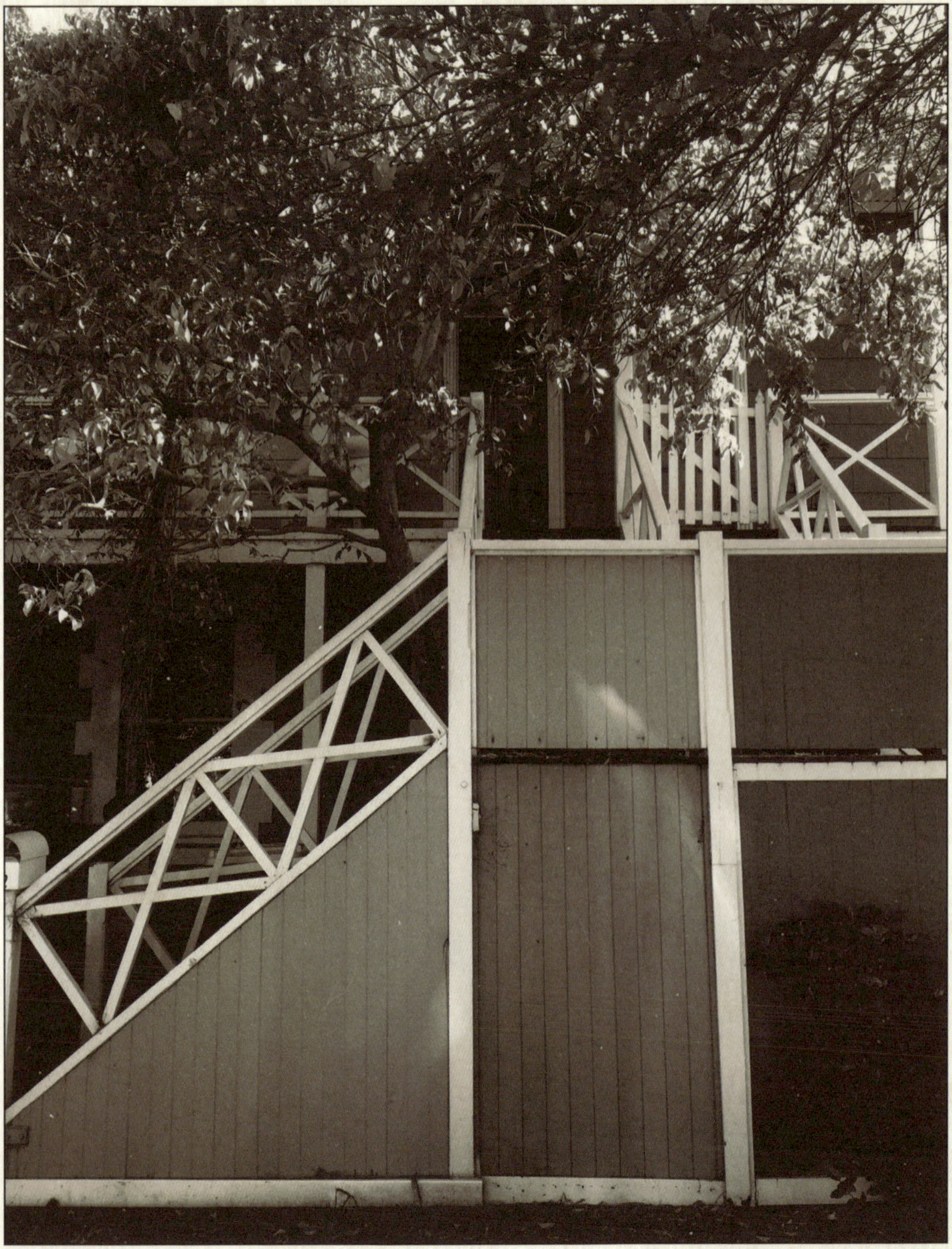

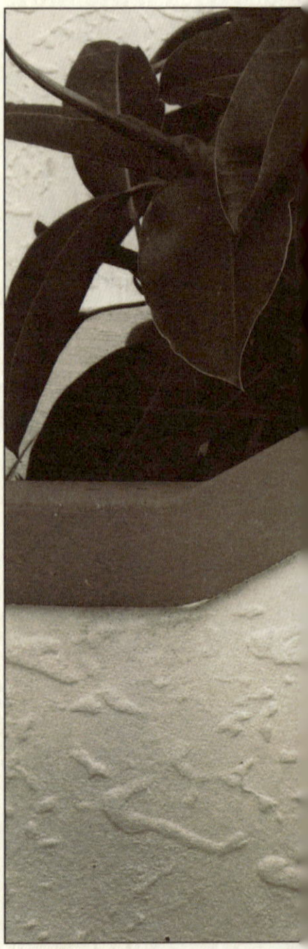

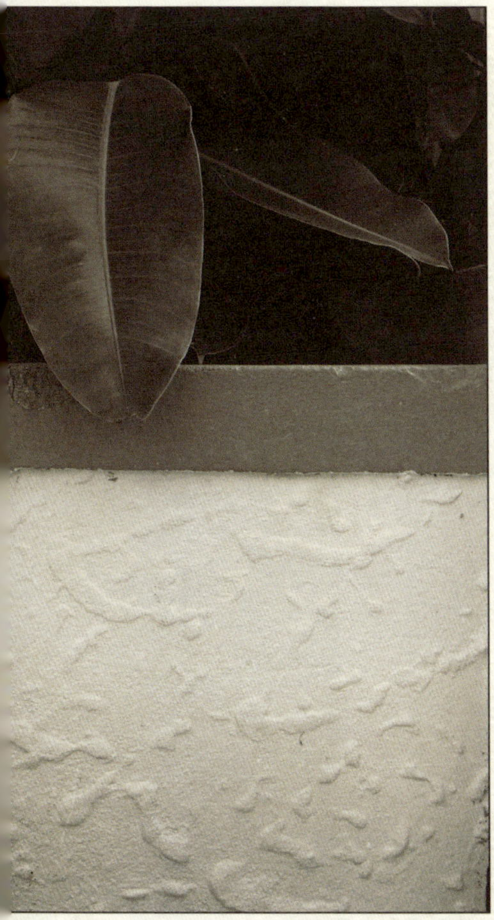

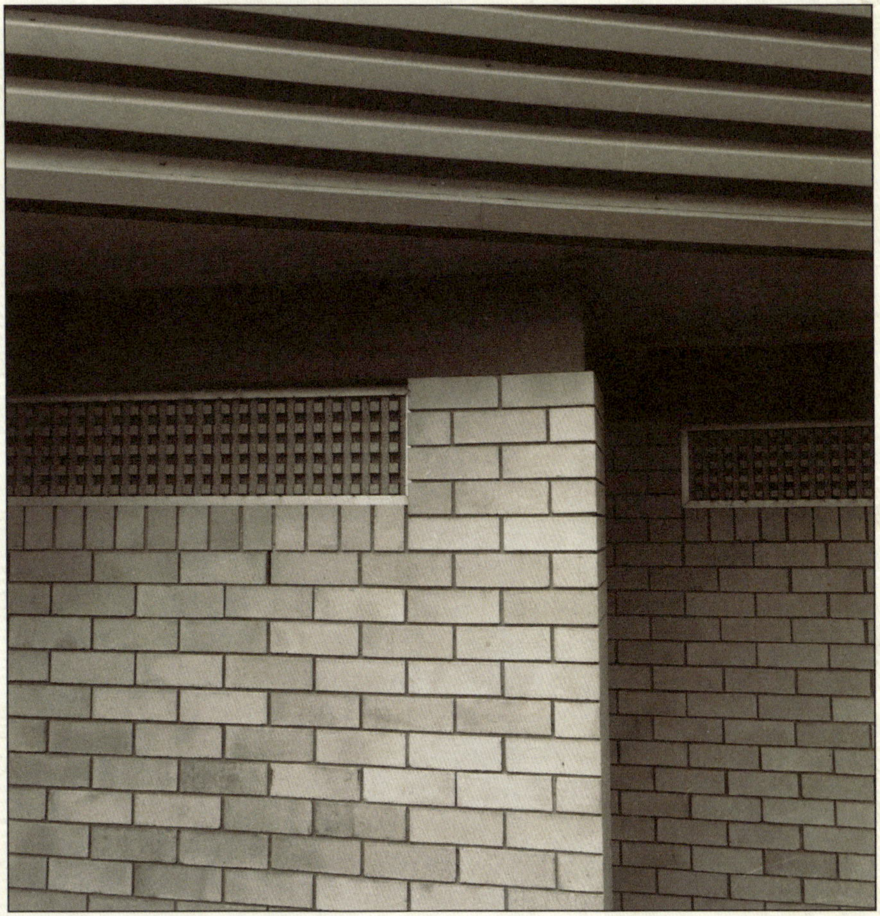

CHAPTER 8

The Beach House

Brett was waiting for me at the bus stop with his Dad when I arrived. A couple of hours before, Mum had dropped me on the highway near the cinema. The coach was idling and I watched the cranky bus driver in shorts and long socks carelessly throw my bag underneath. I passed the time on board by listening to my Walkman and glancing back at the five girls who were three rows behind me on the back seat. I wanted to be that guy who said something witty and was suddenly sitting amongst them, being a total card and having them in stitches with my hilarious anecdotes. Instead I looked out the window, disappointed in myself for not talking to them.

Our family rarely went away during the summer holidays. For a couple of years we'd lobbed at the Rosebud Caravan Park for a few days with some extended family. My youngest cousin Sarah was four and always seemed to be chewing green bubble gum. Everyone thought she was stealing money and buying Hubba Bubba at the little kiosk, but she vigorously denied it. After we grilled her, we were all walking down the road through the caravans and annexes towards the beach when we caught her chewing again. Her sister screamed at her.

"Where did you get that gum, Sarah?"

"It's everywhere!..."

She picked up a well-chewed and discarded piece off the road, pulled out a few pieces of gravel and popped it in her mouth.

Brett's family had rented a house for two weeks overlooking the beach at Phillip Island. The last time I had been there was during a primary school excursion to see the fairy penguins surf the waves in at night and waddle across the beach and up into the dunes to feed their hungry babies. It wasn't a particularly sophisticated operation in those days. We sat there freezing on the dunes on rickety benches and when the first wave of birds came in they cranked up the fluoros and spotlights and lit up the beach like the Normandy landing. Then the poor

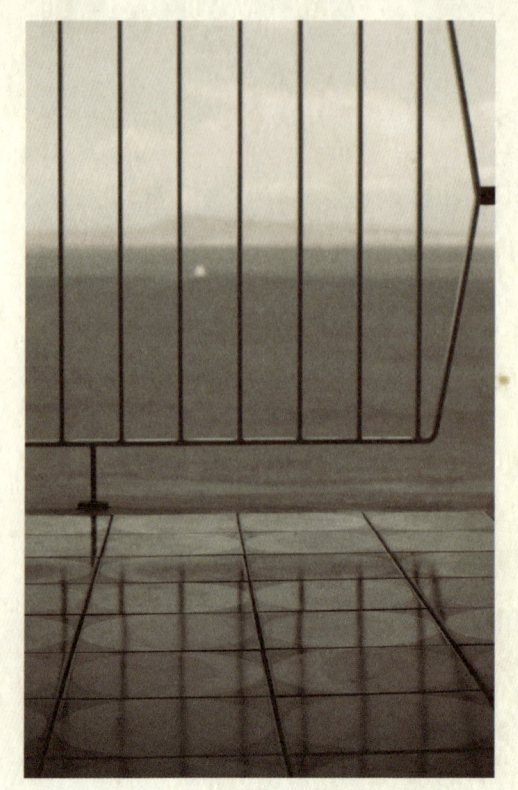

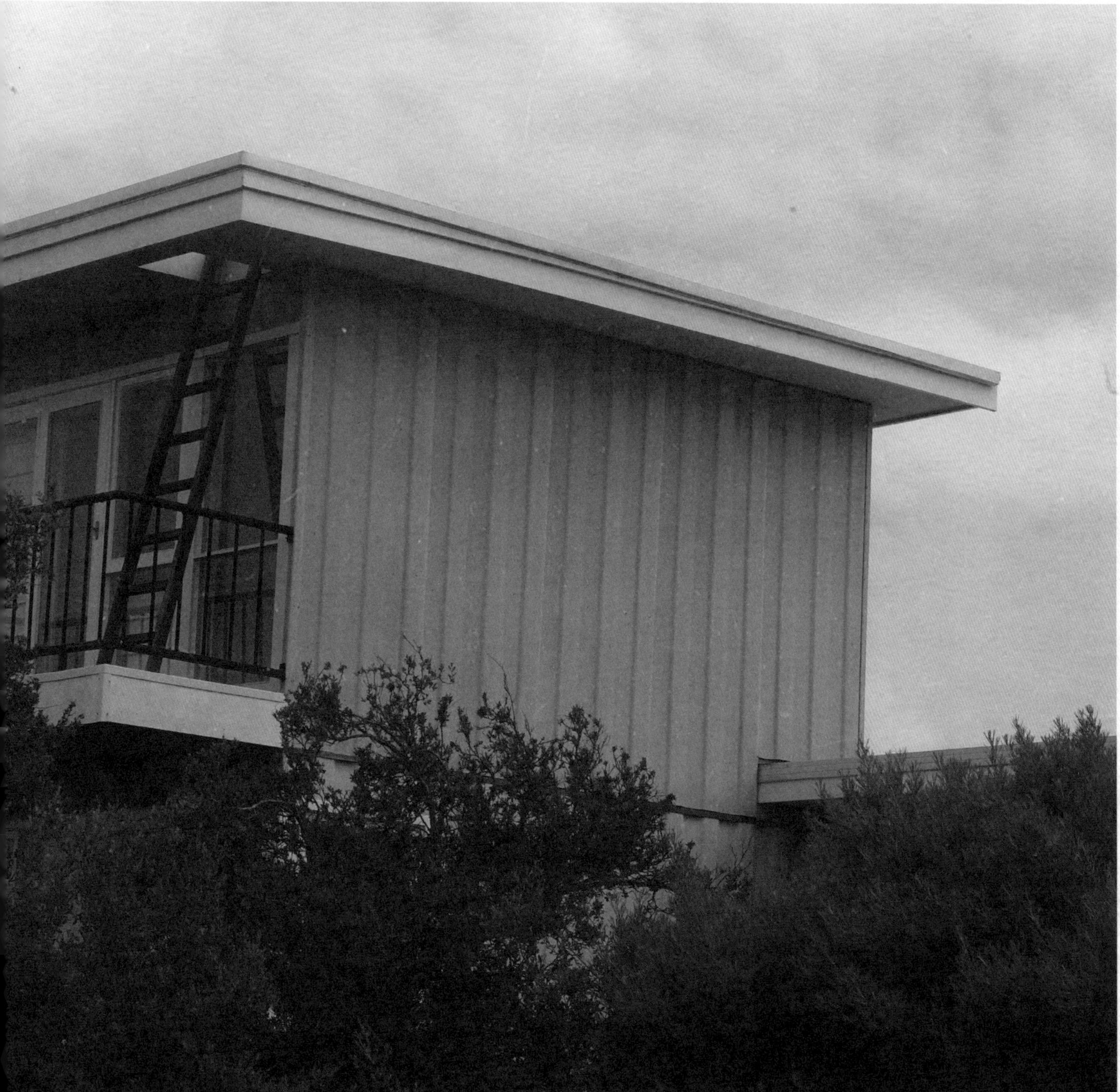

little penguins, exhausted from days at sea, had to dodge the flashbulbs from the Kodak Instamatics and little hands trying to feed them salt and vinegar chips.

Brett was a beanpole who had a habit of dropping his left shoulder so he didn't feel so tall in a crowd, which made him look like he had a hunch. We'd bonded over David Bowie and our shared belief that the legal studies teacher was a fuckwit. Almost every class he'd stand up the front with his beer gut hanging over grey Farah slacks and tell us how he didn't believe in deodorant and that it was a waste of money. "I'll show you my deodorant," he'd say, and draw a shitty picture of a piece of soap on the board. He may have believed it, but the soap didn't. As soon as it hit twenty-five degrees, as sure as there was dandruff on his shoulders, his underarms would start to weep and the smell would make the front two rows of his class a no-go zone.

His archrival was the new geography teacher who had stolen the First XI cricket coaching gig from him. He had recently arrived from South Africa and would lecture anyone who would care to listen that he had moved to Australia to avoid his children going to school with black people. One lunchtime while we were kicking the footy on the oval, someone miskicked the ball and it hit him on the back of the head. I was the first one he saw laughing and he held a grudge against me for the next two years. During the Year 12 cricket season I talked myself into the captaincy of the 3rd XI and used my cricketing wisdom to bowl myself as much as possible. One Saturday morning against a school with a worse sporting reputation than our own, I had good day on the mats bowling off-spinners to some very ordinary batsmen and managed to snare a few off two overs. When reading out the best figures in assembly the geography teacher/cricket coach mumbled "Tim Ross 5/7" out the side of his mouth as quickly as he could.

One of the better cricketers at my school was Doodles. He was an all-rounder who had the potential to play at the highest level but not the commitment. After our school years were over, he chose to stay playing with hangovers in the local league rather than have a crack at the big time. He performed well and was chosen to play in a Country XI against the Victorian Sheffield Shield side. One of the shield players was Shane Warne. When Warnie was bowling, Doodles, sitting on a bench near the pavilion, told his teammates that he thought Warnie was overrated. When the next wicket fell Doodles put on his gloves, picked up his bat and declared, "Watch this, I'm going to tonk Warnie for six, first ball."

He went out to the middle, took centre and calmly waited for Warnie to come in to bowl. Warnie ran in and let fly with a top spinner and Doodles danced down the pitch and hit him straight back over his head for six. He ran around with his bat in the air like he'd made a century and his teammates went ballistic. When he finally composed himself he took block again and waited for Warnie's next delivery. Again he danced down the pitch, eyes focused, bat in the air ready to swat. The ball hit the pitch, Doodles unleashed a mighty swing, missed completely and it crashed into the stumps.

Brett's holiday house was perched on treated pine stilts on a clear grass block one street back from the beach. It was a classic Australian beach house, owner-built over years with a mismatch of materials bought, borrowed and stolen. The outside walls were a mess of odd bits of timber and ill-fitting asbestos sheets. Upstairs was a simple pine kitchen, separated from the living/dining area by a large island bench. The main bedroom and bathroom were upstairs and a large balcony jutted out the front where aluminum folding chairs with fraying webbed seats sat on the cracked and weathered decking. Downstairs was an outside bathroom/laundry and a large bunkroom with a ping-pong table. A variety of different curtains hung from the walls and an old piece of musty brown carpet with rolled-up edges did the job of covering the floor. This was going to be our domain for the next week.

Brett was an only child and had all the toys in the world to prove it. He had brought with him the spoils of his Christmas: a portable CD player, surfboard, boogie board and a tan Top Gun-esque leather jacket. He was wearing the jacket when they picked me up from the bus stop. He asked me if I liked it and I lied and said yes; he smiled and then told me I wasn't allowed to wear it. I didn't care; it was thirty-two degrees outside, plus it was three sizes too big for me and looked like it was from Target.

Brett was still reeling from being unfairly accused for a school crime he didn't commit. At the start of Term 3 somebody sent the French teacher a rather ribald letter to which she rightly took offence. A full-scale covert operation was put into swing and the Deputy Headmaster instructed all students in Year 10 and above to write a one-page essay on footy. They then had a handwriting sample of each one of the boys so they could make a match and find the culprit.

By lunchtime the real reason we had written the essay had leaked. The school was abuzz with theories and somehow the finger was pointed at Brett. He protested but the chatter became so strong that even the teachers decided he was the prime suspect. His essay was the first to be dug out and compared but he was immediately struck off the list due to his inability to spell 'because'. This didn't stop him from being guilty in the schoolyard and the taunts were relentless. His cause wasn't helped by the Deputy Headmaster failing to find a handwriting match. It turned into a large-scale mystery. Then two weeks later, Mr. Grayson the art teacher returned from long service leave. He walked into the staff room, took one look at the letter and declared, "That's Tony's handwriting!" Tony was the science teacher. Tony started packing up his things straight away.

Brett's parents started every day of our holiday with fried eggs on toast and Bloody Marys and then drank steadily for the rest of the day. They ran a local carpet business and were taking a break from spending every day at the office together by slowly getting drunk every day at the beach together. He watched the cricket and she speed-read Jackie Collins novels from morning till night and the only noise that could be heard all day was the sound of the cricket on the TV and the clinking of ice in glasses.

The house, an insulation-free sweatbox, was like a sauna by 10am. They'd keep the windows and curtains drawn until sundown as the sun would pound the house like a boxer who wouldn't stay down. In the early evening they would finally open up the windows and doors and let the cool breeze flow in straight off the beach.

Every day we'd head to beach and Brett would pretend he could surf and I'd bodysurf and get dumped by waves. We doused ourselves in Reef Coconut Oil and lay face down on scratchy towels and looked at boobs out of the corners of our eyes. We'd spend all day at the beach letting the

Reef Coconut Oil speed up the burning process and then drag our red, salty and sandy bodies up the hill and through the dunes on the treated pine boards chained together along the path that took us back to the holiday house.

By then his folks well and truly had their buzz on. They would fire up the barbecue and we'd eat sausages, potato salad and tinned corn. They happily let us help ourselves to the beers in the fridge and Brett and I would sit on the balcony sharing a longneck listening to the crash of the waves. Brett openly fantasised about how the next day we'd finally meet a bunch of girls at the beach. It would always start with "Imagine this…" and then he'd take me through some ridiculous scenario where a gorgeous girl would stop to talk to him about the book he was reading, which was *Rambo*, based on the hit movie. And then before he knew it she was lying down on a towel next to him and he'd be putting Reef Coconut Oil all over her. She'd invite him back to her parentless holiday house and they'd get in the spa and it would be on like Donkey Kong. I hated his idiotic visions, not only because they were clearly absurd, but because he was the only one who ever got any action in these scenarios. He completely wrote me out of the script.

After a couple of nights hanging out at the house we decided to chance our arm and try and get into the pub. We did our best to get our look on with a pre-metrosexual cocktail of Macleans toothpaste, hair gel and Jazz aftershave. In his shit-brown leather jacket Brett looked at least nineteen and I had my brother's paper licence, so we managed to waltz into the venue without any problems. It was a few days before New Years and the place was heaving. Luckily we bumped into a few people we knew from our area and suddenly we had a little crew going. We drank beers and ouzo and cokes and were impressed by a covers duo who weren't particularly impressive. They wore matching white singlets with superfade jeans and their curly mullets bounced animatedly as they sang 'Run to Paradise' for the third time.

The booze and our sunkissed skin had given us some courage and the holiday spirit had made people friendly and ready to talk. In a stroke of luck I met a pretty girl called Sophie who had private school hair. We were both wearing large Jag t-shirts tucked into oversized peg leg jeans so that gave us a reason to talk. I was instantly smitten.

She was the holiday crush that not even Brett could have dreamt up. She bounced around the pub smiling like she was straight out of a Sportsgirl catalogue and was always carrying a fresh drink that I'm sure she didn't pay for. She would stop on her laps around the venue and we'd share another joke about couple dressing. She lived in Brighton, her parents owned a holiday house on the island and she had the air of someone expecting a hatchback for her eighteenth birthday. She was scatty and I couldn't keep her attention for long. We'd be talking and she would suddenly dart off when a song she liked was being played or she spotted someone new to talk to. I tried following her a few times but she would just keep moving, weaving in and out, always looking for a new mini adventure. They called last drinks, the fluoro lights came on and Sophie disappeared. Brett and I grabbed a bag full of fried dim sims to share and we battled it out with everyone else to get a cab home.

The next day we couldn't wait to do it all again. When we arrived, they had amped up security and Brett got asked for ID. I walked away with him out of solidarity even though the bouncer had let me go in. We walked up the street and saw some guys jumping the fence into the beer garden. Brett went with them, I went back in the other way and we met at the bar a few minutes later. I kept looking around for Sophie and then I saw her talking to a guy in his early twenties who was built to talk to her. He had all shades of good-looking covered and she was fluttering everything she could at him. I didn't bother to go and say hi. At one stage I did bump into her but it was awkward. I struggled for things to say and was almost relieved when she moved on. I found myself talking to her friend Sarah near the cigarette machine. Sarah was sporty and super cute but she wasn't Sophie. We chatted easily and at every opportunity I managed to swing the conversation back to Sophie until the inevitable happened.

"You like her don't you?"

I nodded. I had been baiting her, looking for intel, desperately wanting her to give me an angle, a sliver of hope.

"Well she likes Seb."

She pointed to the tall good-looking Country Road model I'd seen her talking to before. It really sunk in. All the couple-dressing jokes in the world weren't going to compete with a man who had a car, job and fully developed underarm hair. Dejected, I grabbed Brett and we went home.

The next night was New Year's Eve and Brett's folks had struck up a friendship with the couple next door. They spent all their time baking themselves and looked like a couple of goannas in bathers. He mowed the lawn in his thongs every second day and she chainsmoked cigarettes and fed biscuits to her Jack Russells. Apparently they'd moved the beer fridge from the garage into the lounge room to make life easier, so it was no surprise they'd all hit if off.

We left them drinking and headed down early to make sure we could get into the pub. It was buzzing, cars were piled up around the corner waiting to get into the drive-through bottle shop. Bag after bag of ice was dropped on the concrete, freeing it up so it could slide easily into Eskys. We managed to score a table in the beer garden and our crew quickly had it covered with jugs of beer. I was adamant that I wouldn't look around for Sophie, and had just convinced myself it was time to move on when she sat down next to me. She looked amazing and somehow had given herself an extra boost to her private school hair. She was talking to me about something to do with the beach but I didn't hear a word of it. I was deep in a pile of teen attraction and I wasn't getting out. Just when I thought she would leave, she didn't. She stayed and listened to me and laughed when I told her Brett

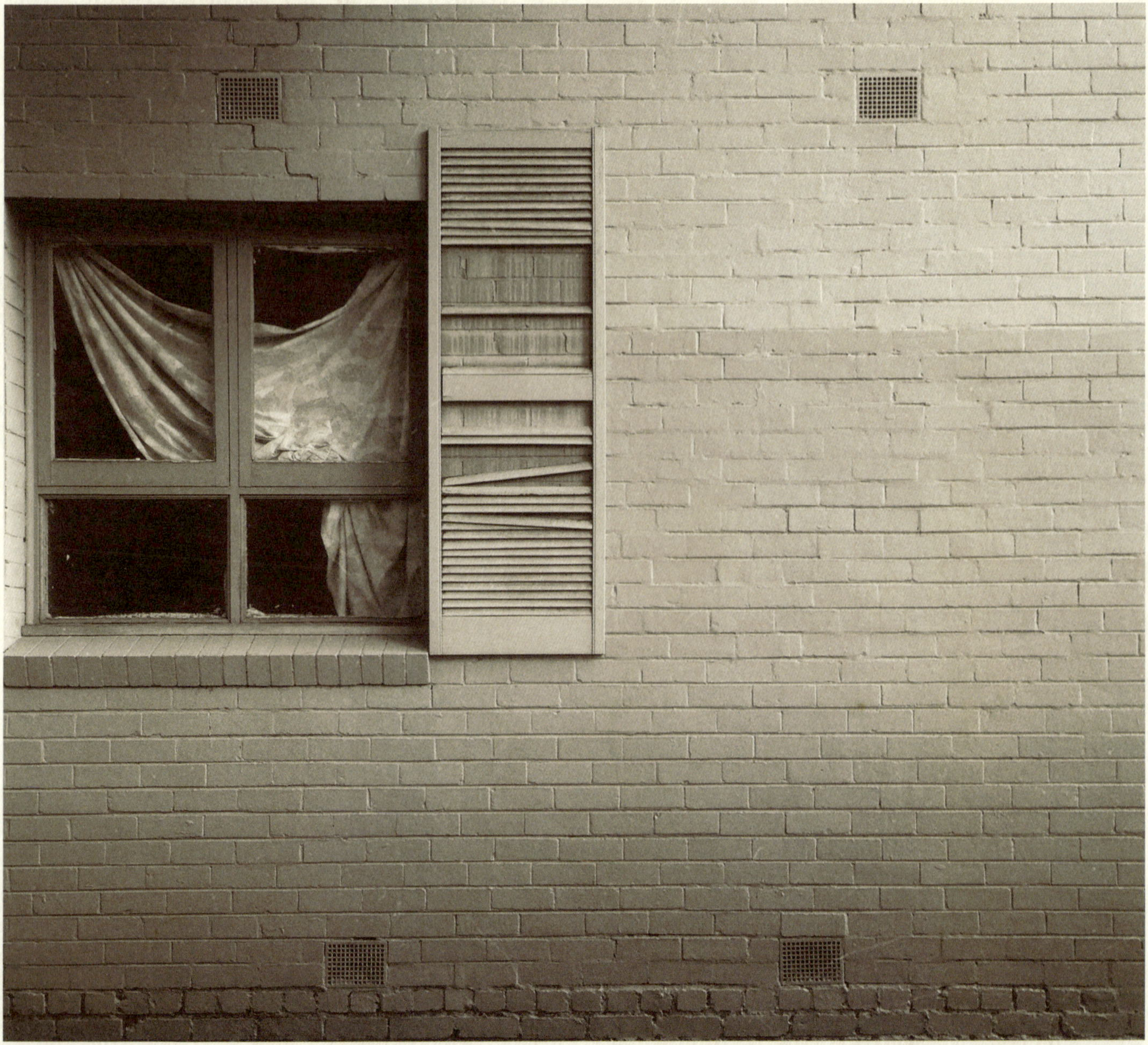

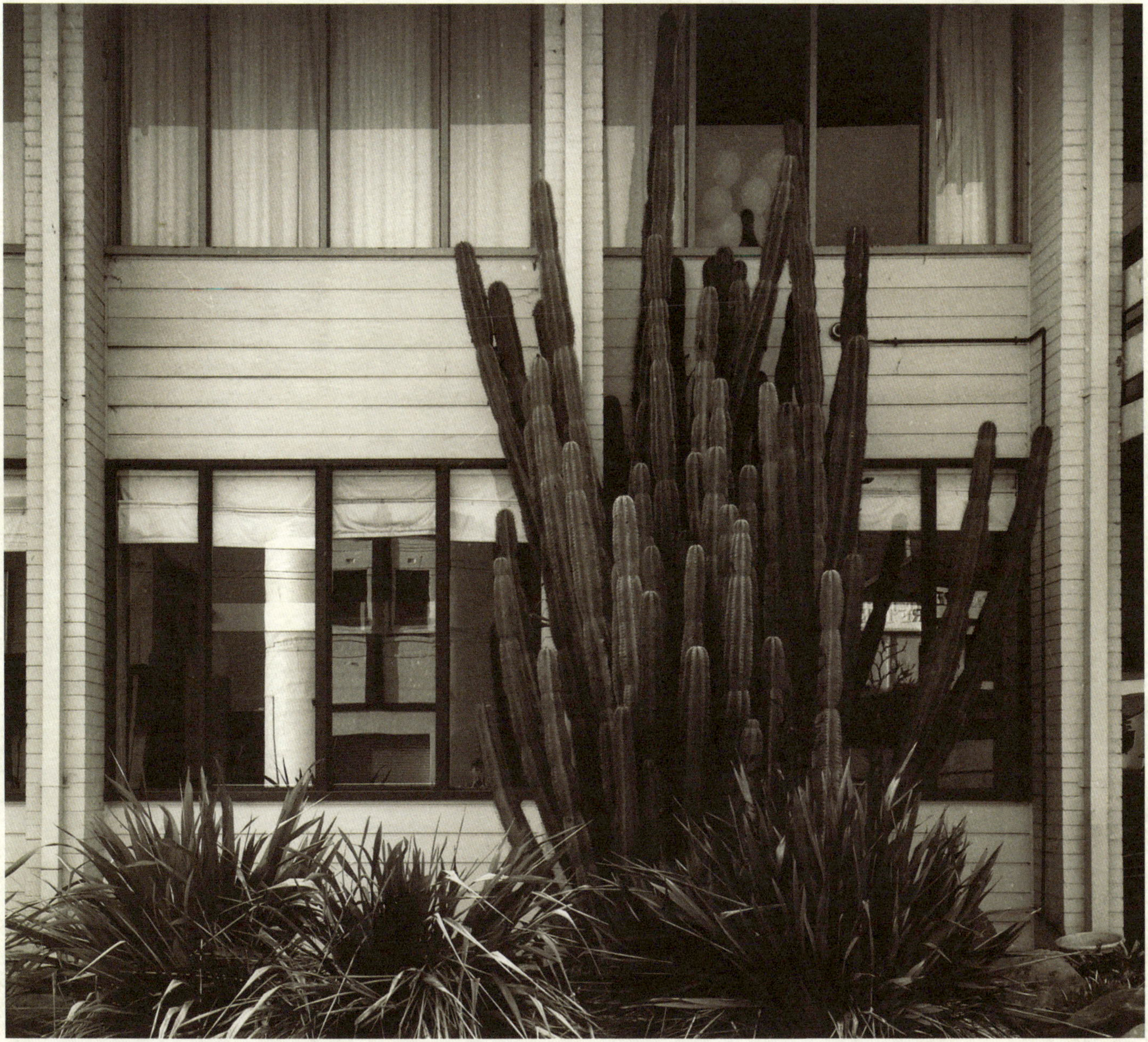

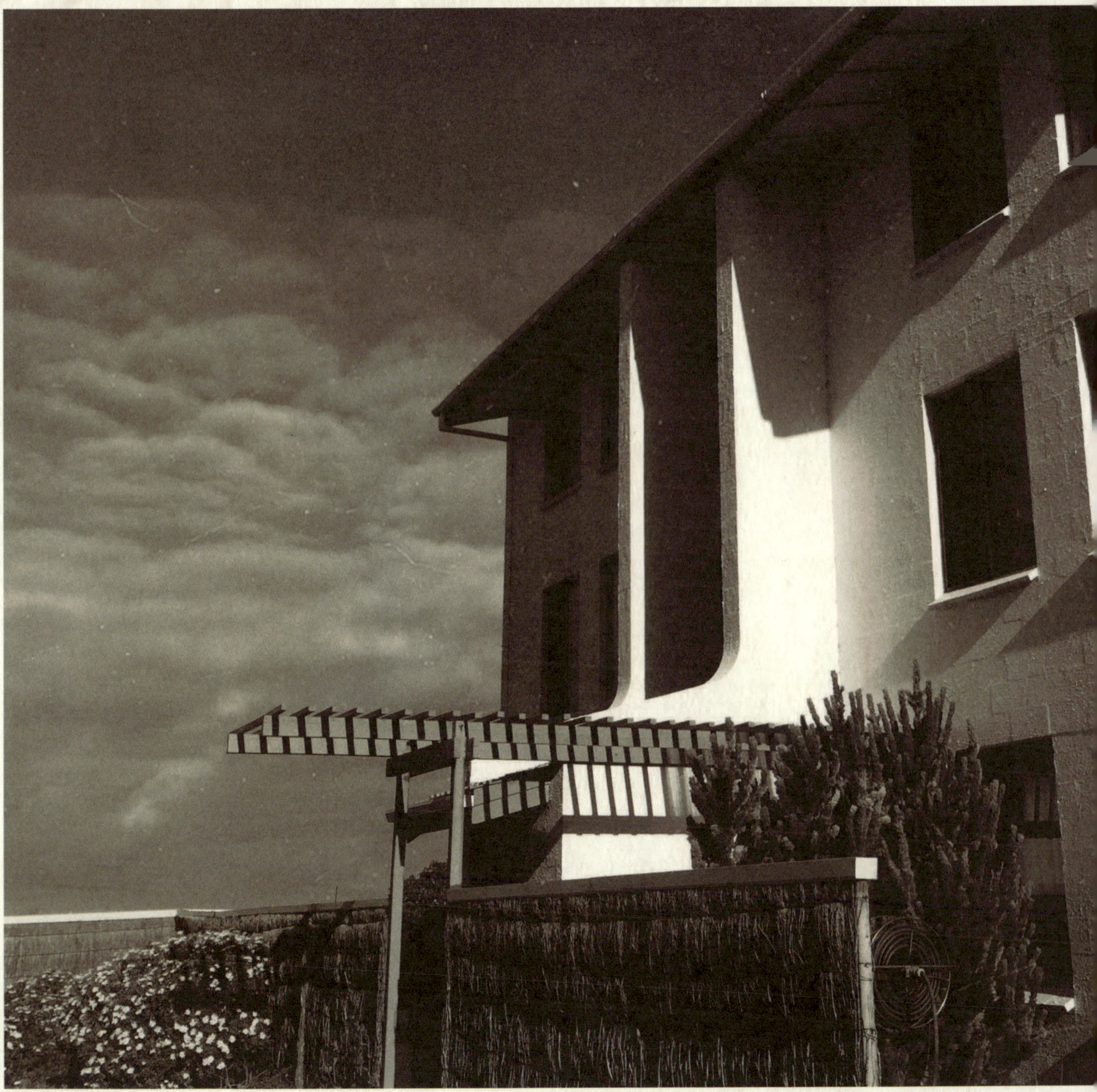

once wore his Mum's perfume to a blue light disco thinking it was aftershave.

I'd had quite a few beers and desperately needed to go the bathroom. I waited until the final moment before I pissed my pants, excused myself and bolted to the gents. When I returned she was on the other side of the beer garden talking to the Country Road model and his mates who wore matching shit-eating Toyota Rav 4-driving grins and were drinking Slippery Nipples like A-grade fuckwits. They were men, I was barely seventeen and there was no chance of any *Karate Kid*-style heroics from me. I went back to the table, defeated.

Brett had met a twenty-six year old single mum from Cranbourne and bullshitted that he played under-nineteens footy for Carlton. By the time the countdown started they were sucking face at the bar and he had one hand up her top and the other trying to dismantle her high-waisted acid wash jeans. Luckily the bouncers intervened before it got too disgusting and they pushed everyone out of the venue.

I lost my crew in the swarm down to the beach and was standing there alone contemplating going home. I knew Brett would be in a caravan by now, desperately trying not to wake a baby. It was a near-full moon in a clear sky. I walked around for a while trying to find someone I knew. After ten minutes I gave up and climbed the steps, where I bumped straight into Sophie, who was also alone, and very drunk. She put her arms around me and slurred "Happy New Year!" and kissed me on the lips. I kissed her back and she kissed me back even more. I could have kissed her more, I wanted to kiss her more, but I walked away, leaving her on the beach. This was not how it was supposed to be. I went back to the holiday house and waited for Brett to make his way home.

CHAPTER 9
The Motel

The kids finally drop their heads and fall asleep amongst the bits of rice cake just as we pull into the Colonial Motor Inn. There are plenty to choose from on the Motel Mile coming into this country town where tonight we will eat Chinese with a fork and a spoon. It's not the best one on the strip, but we don't want the best. We are chasing a motel where the only thing new is the TV in the room and a dangling Foxtel sign out the front.

We want speckled exposed brown brick walls and frosted glass windows above the door that bend and filter the headlights of the latest guests checking in. We are looking for the little door where breakfast will appear hours after we've ticked a box that says Pineapple Juice. The eggs will be poached in aluminium cups in a steamer and the bread will come in a little paper bag. We'll find the toaster in the cupboard next to the plastic Kambrook kettle and I'll sneak one of the sugar-coated biscuits from the twin pack that sits on a caramel-coloured tray.

The thin green towels will be fanned out on the bed, the soap will be in individual white packets and a paper strip will sit over the Caroma toilet.

The compendium will tell us the worst places to eat and have a menu of dinner items that are crumbed, fried, or crumbed and fried.

A brown air conditioner, which blows either too hot or too cold, will whir, splutter and rattle. The clock radio built into the bedhead will flash the wrong time and the alarm will go off at 3am, waking us from our MSG sweats.

We will lie in bed with the electric blanket on and watch an old man and a young woman read the regional news. We'll laugh at the shit ads for farm equipment.

Our two little boys will jump up and down on the bed, so excited to be in this new place. We will be happy because it's what we used to do. It will make us feel safe. It will make us feel at home.

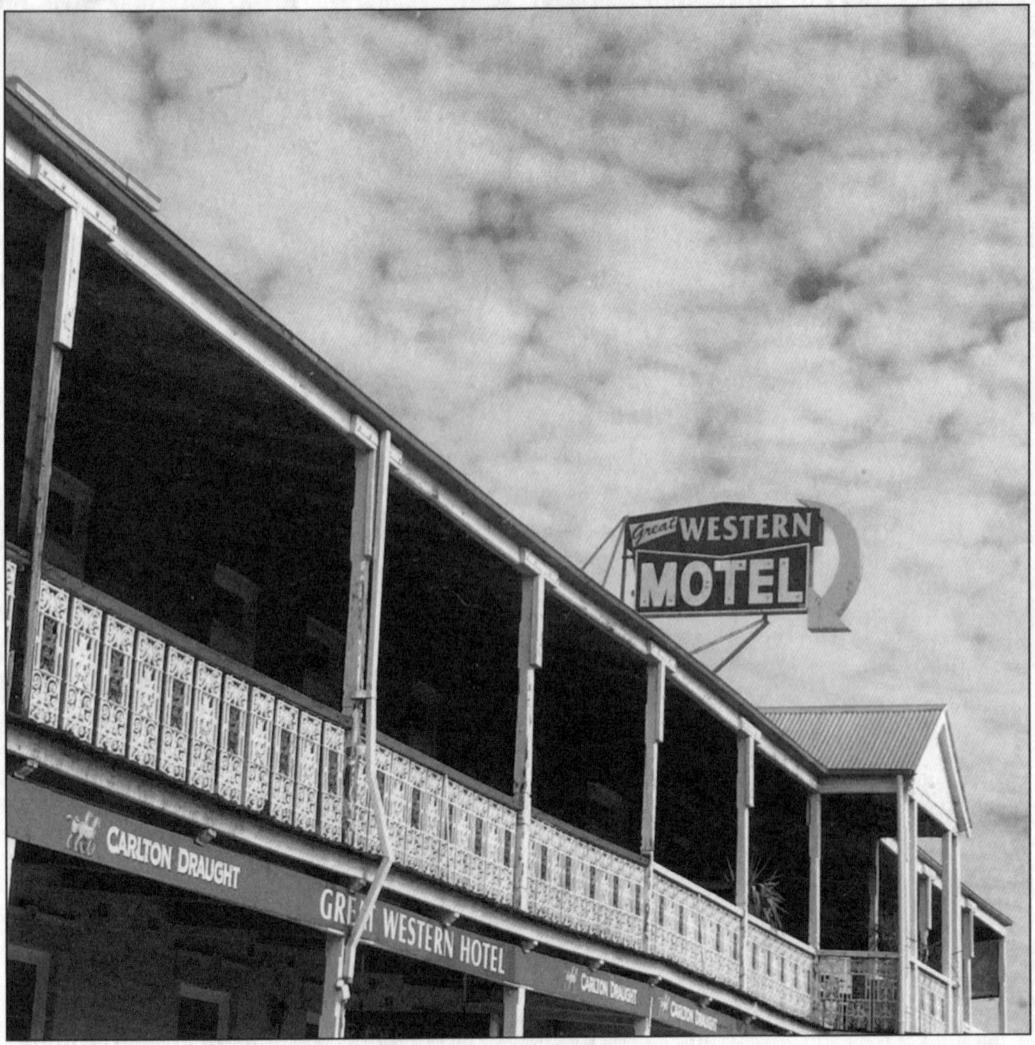
Great WESTERN
MOTEL
CARLTON DRAUGHT

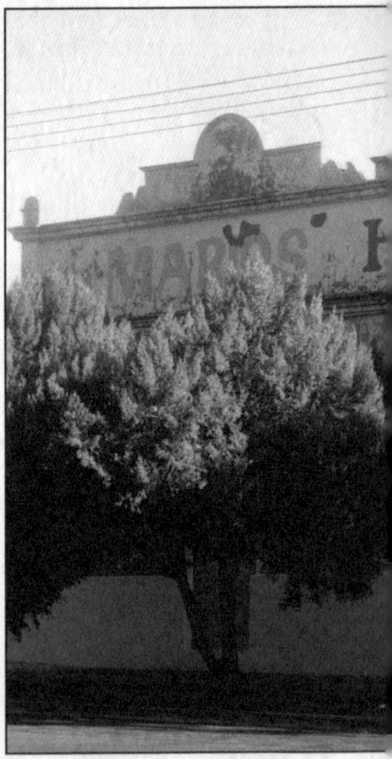

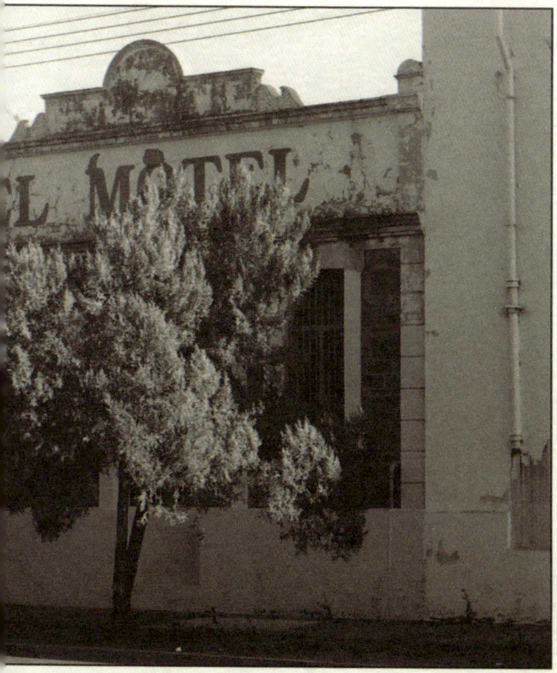

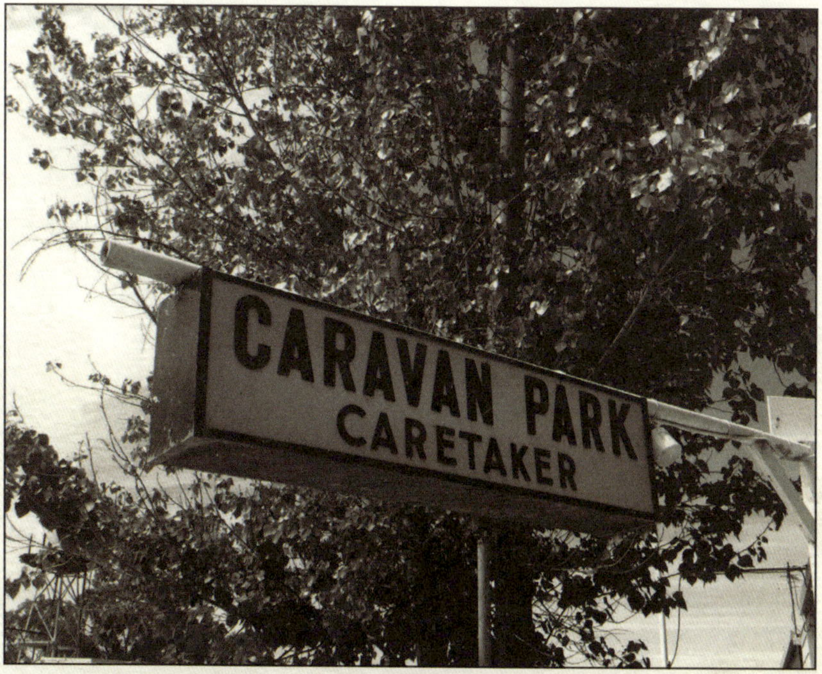
CARAVAN PARK
CARETAKER

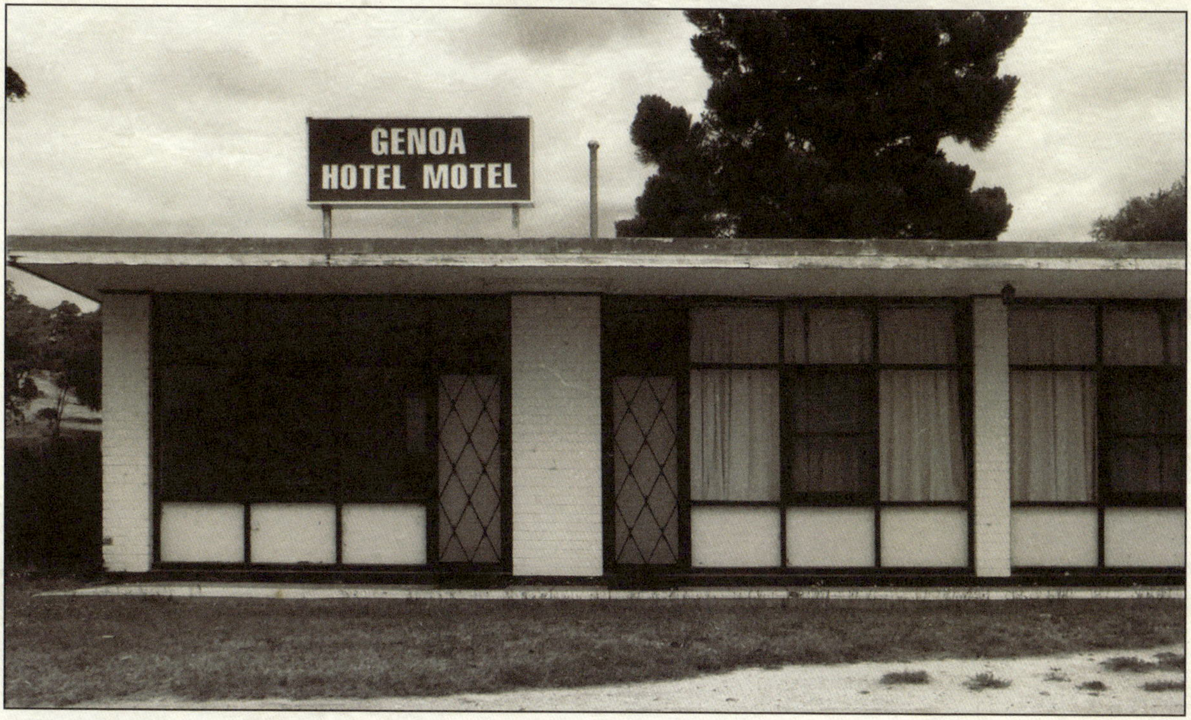
GENOA
HOTEL MOTEL

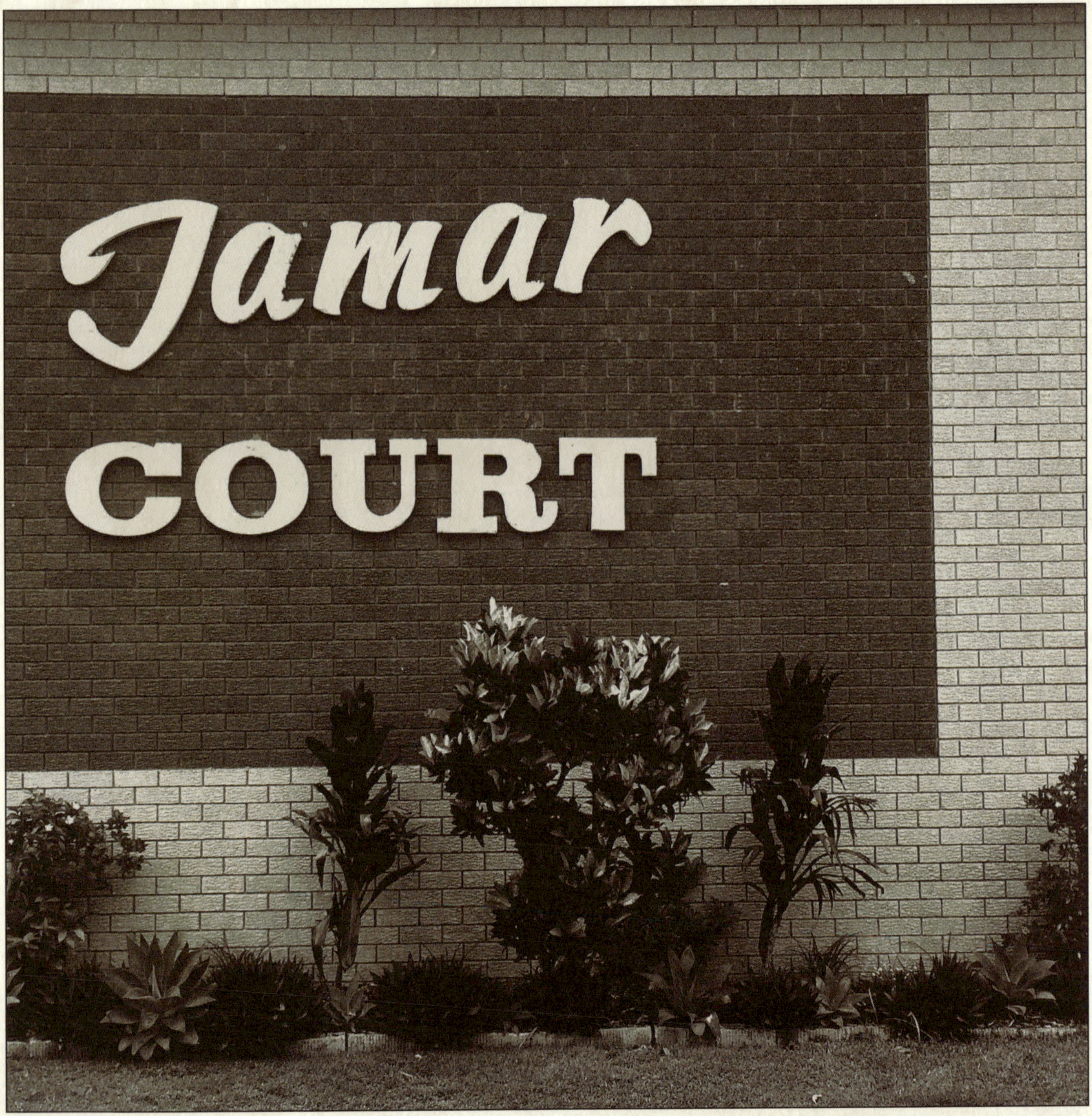
Jamar
COURT

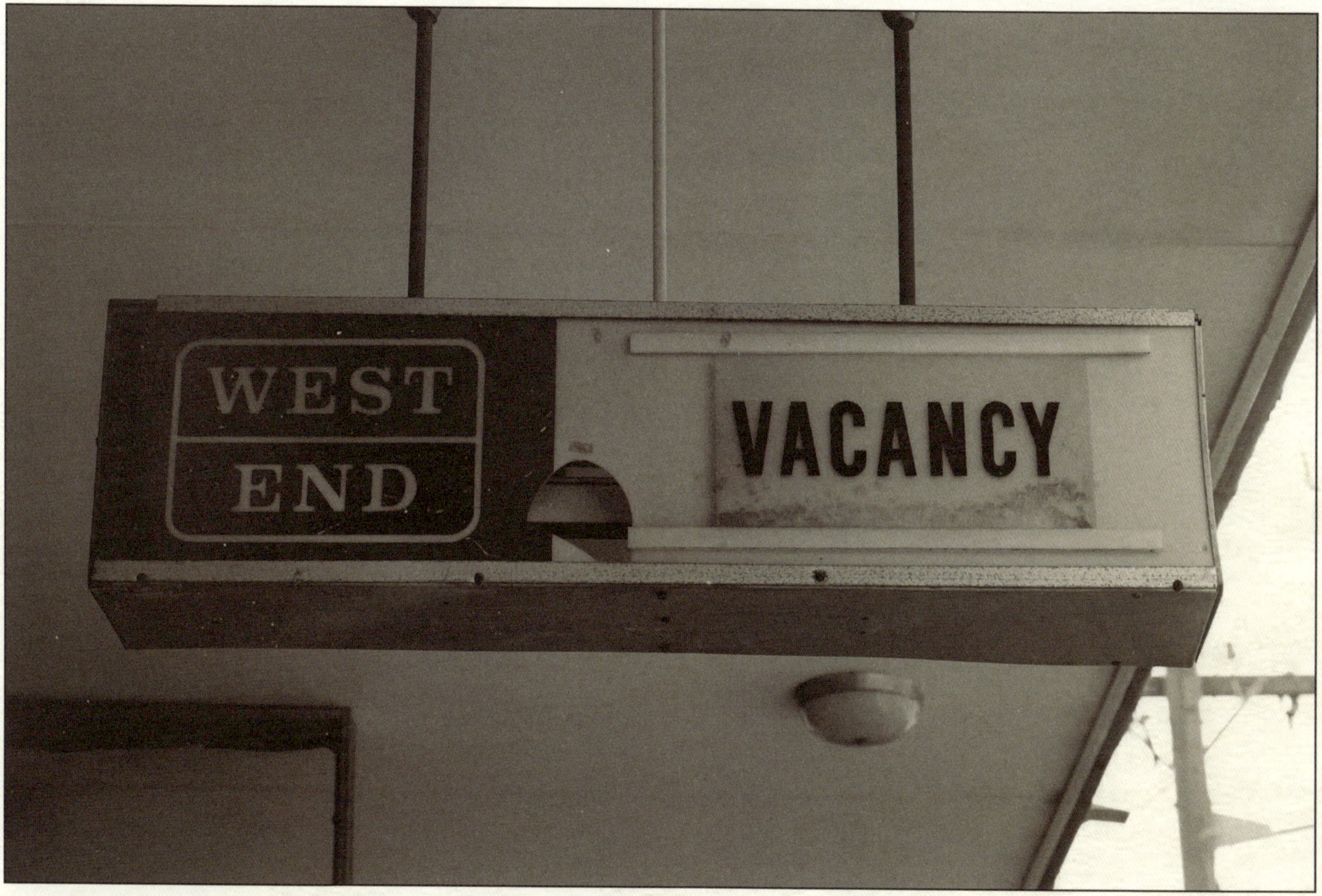
WEST
END
VACANCY

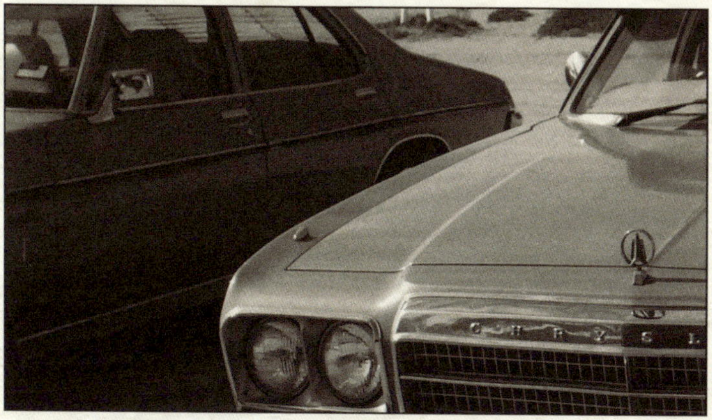

CHAPTER 10

New Horizon

Her new apartment block sat upright, tall and alone. A white sculpture stack of perfectly tied ribbons; a majestic, arrogant Fuck You to a city that hates the interesting. She was mostly immune to its presence; she just liked the view from the inside — all that sparkle and blue, white sails and sprawl.

It was less than a kilometre from her old place, a Deco apartment on the sixth floor, just above the noise from the street and the threat of other people looking into her apartment. She'd happily dragged the last of her stuff into the rickety old lift and across the parquetry floor that had been sanded bare by seventy years of comings and goings.

It had been her home for the last five years and she was sick of the assorted men from her past pushing on the buzzer at 2am in the morning. Men with three hundred dollar bags in the pocket of three hundred dollar jeans. Men who left fake tan stains on her dunny seat.

Sometimes she would let them in if she felt the need but mostly she ignored them and their text messages, leaving them to trudge back along the road to the flashing lights and pizza slices.

Now she was on the fifteenth floor, completely away from the action, in an apartment full of cookbooks that she would never use. She told some friends that it was her uncle's apartment and that she got cheap rent; she told others that it was her own. Somewhere in between still wasn't the truth.

She sat on the carpet eating tuna on rice cakes and drinking white wine. Just down the hill a divorcee in her new apartment had answered the buzzer curiously and was now bent over the bed enjoying the spoils of the former tenant.

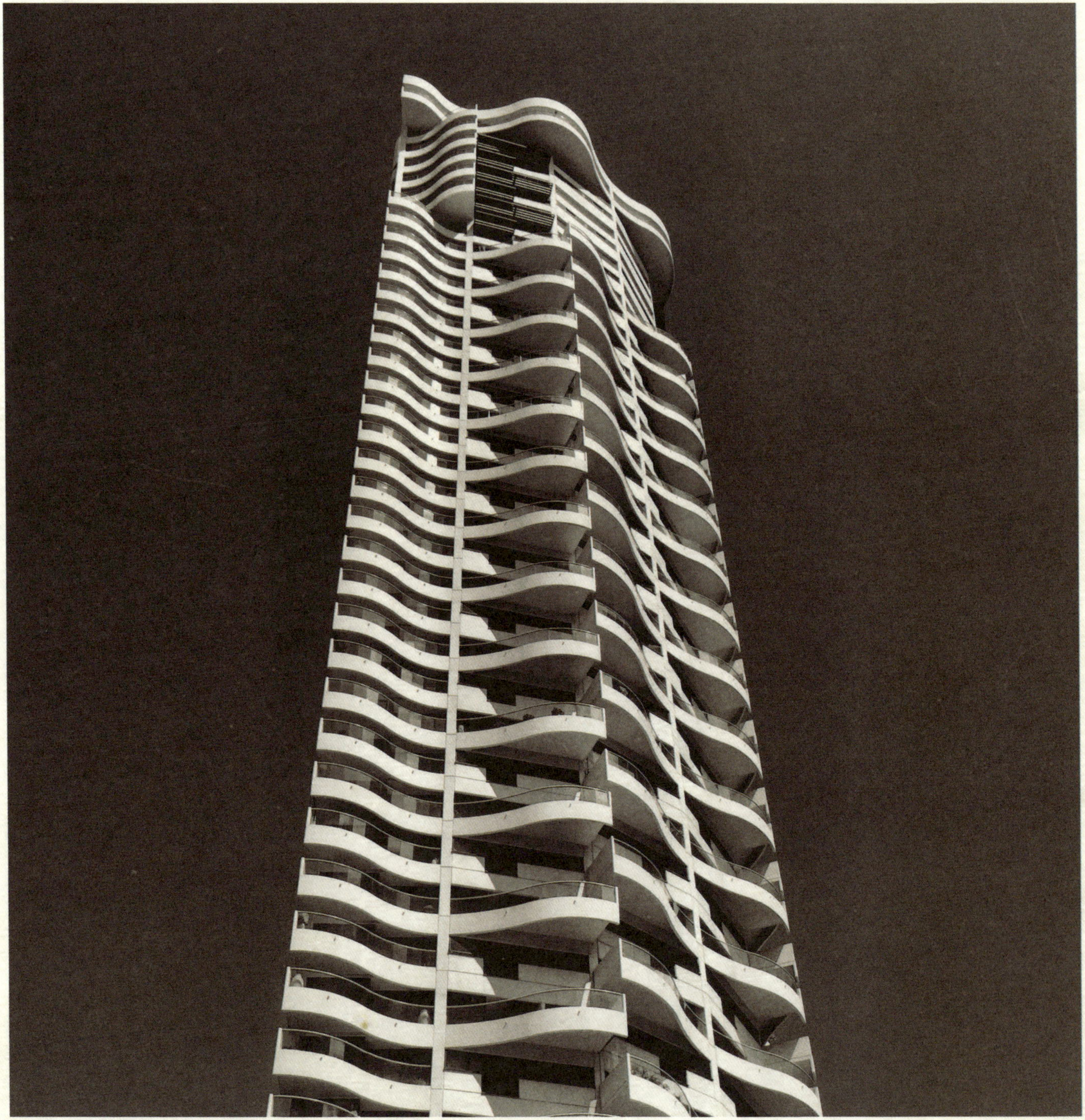

CHAPTER 11

It's a Shame About Rae's

He could only find one thong so scratching his waxed chest out of habit he decided to go down to the beach in bare feet. He walked down the brick driveway and saw where he had butted his smoke out on the pandanus tree the night before while he watched her spew Pinot Gris and Sri Lankan curry all over the gutter. As he walked past, a brush turkey boldly breakfasted on the bits of regurgitated yellow Balmain bug meat.

The surf was flat at Wategos. There was just a solitary white campervan parked at the end of the road. Its tanned owner was cooking two-minute noodles in a foil oven tray on the public barbecue and didn't look up as he walked down the path, over the rocks and onto the sand where he dropped his white towel. He lamented the lack of waves, but ran down to the water and dived in. Immediately his head cleared, but his balls stung from where he'd cut himself shaving on the wrong side of half a dozen Coronas. He shot out of the water, then when the pain subsided, took himself under again, this time opening his eyes to the green below. He pushed down and along the sand, following a small white fish that darted in and out of the shadows and ripples of light.

He was waiting for the ocean to strip him back, to break the barnacles of stress that dug themselves deep into his shoulders, to cleanse him, to give him a colonic of his fucked-up soul. But nothing budged. The deeper he went, the further he swam, no matter what stroke, a different kind of anger consumed him. Nothing disappeared; the ocean could not weave its magic.

With his towel low-slung around his waist, he walked back up the path and up the road where the brush turkey and curry were both gone. He opened the door to room five and she was lying on the bed pimping photos of herself in a bikini on Instagram for likes.

He silently slipped into the shower and shooed the sand out of the cut on his sack with warm water. He half-dried himself, sprayed some Lynx on and slid into bed with girlfriend number five who he had shared room number four with.

CHAPTER 12

A Couple of Cans on the Back Step

I was fourteen when Craig and Justine moved in next door with their two stupid cocker spaniels, Ben and Sam. Cocker spaniels, like poodles, are the worst dogs in the world, unless you own one. From the moment they arrived they barked constantly, and I was a young man with raging hormones and no room for their shit in my life. Yes, their dangly ears and droopy eyes can be cute but if they are yapping their heads off because they think your school jumper hanging on the clothesline is a wombat, it's pretty easy to see straight through their looks.

All day they ran up and down the fence ready to get angry at anything or anyone that came close, although Craig and Justine said they were just adjusting. They also said they were about to put in a pool and were looking forward to sharing it with us, so we decided that putting up with the dogs was no big deal.

Craig was in his mid-thirties, completely bald on the top of his head but with heavy growth around the sides. He was a sales rep for a soft drink company and drove around in a brand new silver Jaguar. I'd often be walking to school when he was driving to work and he'd give me a lift while I tried not to scuff my school bag against the walnut trim on the dash. We talked about whatever sport was in season and I felt pretty cool getting out of the Jag at the school gates.

They started on the pool almost immediately, but it was hard to track its progress because they built a tall brushwood fence around it. The dogs didn't calm down over time; they stayed exactly the same, if not worse. We put up with it. We were waiting for summer and the grand opening of the pool.

One Thursday night while we were having a dinner of grilled chops, steamed carrots and potatoes microwaved in their jackets, Craig knocked on the back door. They were heading to Lorne for the weekend and he asked if I would mind feeding Ben and Sam while they were away. It didn't seem like much of a stretch, so I said yes. The one thing I didn't like about dog food was when you gave the dog half a can and had to cover the rest and put it in the fridge. No matter what sort of cover you put on, it always stunk it out. I wouldn't have any issues here though, because Ben and Sam would split a can a night.

Craig left the cans on the back step, but when I tried to lower their enamel bowls full of rank gelatinous lumps over the waist-high gate, the dogs fired up and were all snarls and gnashing teeth. They were so aggressive that the next night I didn't bother with their bowls and just spooned the food straight out of the can onto the concrete pavers and let them fight it out. On Sunday night, Craig arrived again at the back door smiling, thanked me profusely and handed me a twenty-dollar note. I was stoked; it was the easiest money I'd ever earned.

The next time he turned up asking me to feed the dogs, it was for three days. I said yes as quick as I could. Banking on another bumper payday I even reverted to putting the food in the bowls out of a sense of professionalism. I couldn't work out how much I'd get this time for the extra day. Would it be thirty? Or maybe he'd splash out and make it forty? Either way I wasn't complaining.

Once again he arrived at the back door smiling, made some small talk with the folks about his time away, then thanked me and left without giving me any money. I was taken aback. Maybe he forgot? Maybe the twenty was for feeding the dogs in perpetuity? It wasn't like I could go and ask him.

A month later it was stinking hot day and Ben and Sam were barking at me again while I pulled what they thought was a wombat off the clothesline. Behind the brushwood fence I could hear Craig and Justine splashing in the pool.

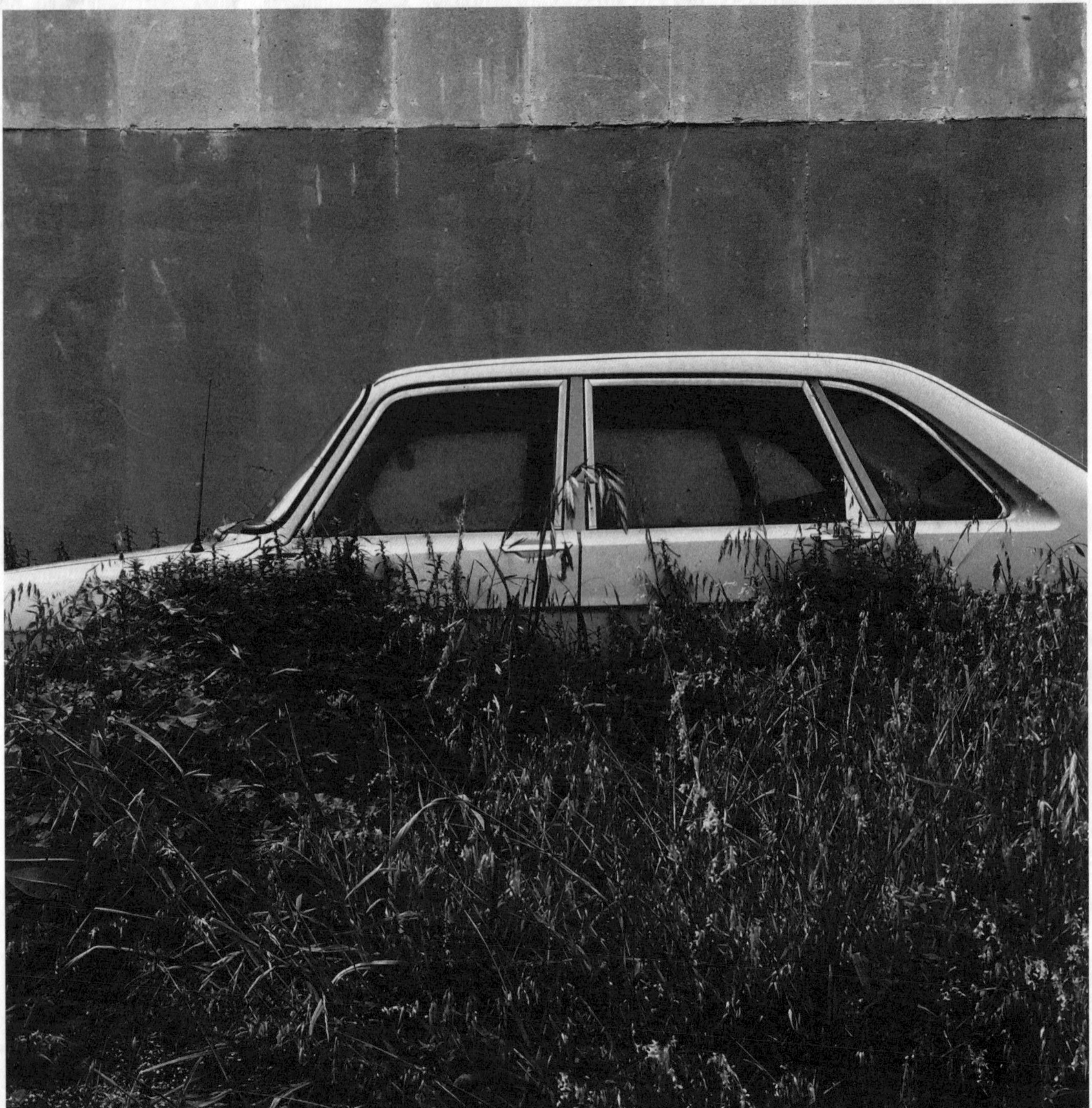

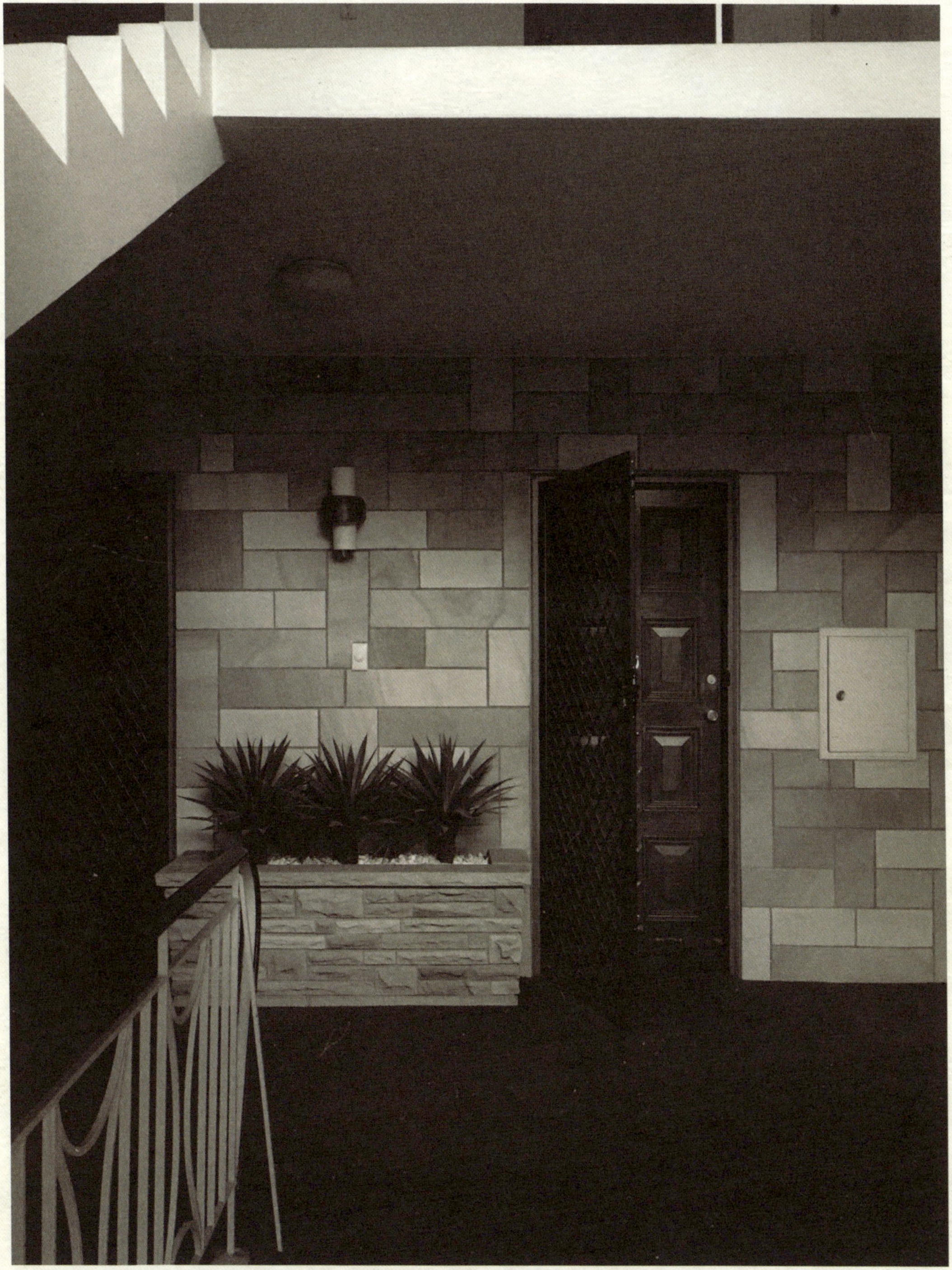

CHAPTER 13

The Terrace House Strikes Back

It was the year everyone seemed to be eating wedges with sweet chilli sauce and doing it to Jeff Buckley. They put on mid-nineties 'doing it' faces and anecdotally there was some very melodramatic pumping going on to his album *Grace*. I wasn't part of this movement. Not because I didn't like Jeff Buckley; I loved Jeff Buckley and would have been bang-up for making it my soundtrack and turning my bedroom antics into a bad audition for NIDA, but unfortunately I didn't own a CD player.

Since my final year at school I couldn't wait to get out of the suburbs and into the city. All that space I'd loved as a kid was suddenly alienating and I craved density. I wanted to be part of the action. The great symbol of that action was the terrace house. These old buildings that were left for dead in the sixties and seventies came back like Lazarus when a generation of Australians turned their backs on our great sprawling suburbs and came back to the city looking for action, just like I was.

I often wondered what the long-gone former residents would have made of the shenanigans that happened in some of the inner-city sharehouses I lived in. Imagine being of a time when the most outrageous thing you'd seen was someone doing the Charleston, and then a guy in a bad Kurt Cobain haircut, undies and a pair of Moon Boots was pulling a cone through a Star Trek bong in the room you used to sit in with your family and listen to radio plays. How could you fathom seeing your bedroom, where you lay awake at night worried about how you were going to buy shoes for your kids (well you would have if you weren't so tired from lugging coal), now being the venue for some pagan-looking ritual where two people fucked to Jeff Buckley?

It seemed there was a lot of action up for grabs, only I kept missing it. In my second year of uni I balked at doing a performance subject because I thought it was a complete arty wank. So as pretty as the girls were, I ran a mile when discussions started taking place about how to make an already-dull play twice as boring, and as a result I wasn't part of a production that led to what was known as the best cast party of all time.

86

The production itself involved twenty girls running around in cheesecloth dresses pretending to be trees and rolling over the two lucky guys who were the only men in the cast. Lana, one of the leads, wore dark eye makeup, had hair like a bird's nest and thought showering was a multiple choice question. Despite her bare feet and hippy vibe, she came from a wealthy family and her Dad had bought her a mud brick home in the bush. It had five bedrooms, which she filled with people paying good rent, and was making a fortune out of her 'commune'. She smoked rollies, couldn't say anything without gesturing like she was in a yoga class and had terrible eczema from her henna tattoos, but was sort of hot in that 'I can see your side boob while you sit on the grass and eat a lentil patty' kind of way. It was at her house that the party happened. Where everyone ended up nude in the pool. Where everyone kissed each other and more. Where I was sitting at home in the terrace eating spag bol made from pet-quality mince with whoever was living in the front room at the time.

When I moved in Jerry had been there for a year. He worked at the Commonwealth Bank as a teller and worked out you could steal two dollars a day without anyone caring or noticing. Every day he slipped a two dollar coin into his grey slacks, which he then put in a large VB tin money box. He would never drink during the week but on Friday night he would write himself off with his workmates and then lie on the couch eating chicken and chips for two days until it was time to go to work again. He didn't talk much but wasn't awkward to be around. As long as he had enough Corn Flakes to eat and could steal money from the bank he was smiling. One Saturday he didn't have a hangover and instead opened his money box, went to JB Hi-Fi, bought himself a brand-new colour TV and packed all his stuff into his car. "This place is fucked, I'm moving back in with Mum and Dad," was all he said. And then he was gone.

I was tempted to move from my room out the back, which was a brick tack-on, into his bigger room at the front, but it was ten bucks more a week. At one stage mushrooms had started growing through the carpet in my room and I'd blown up at the real estate agent demanding a rent decrease. They sent a bloke out to investigate, which is when we discovered that I hadn't tightened the hose on the washing machine properly and the water was streaming down through the wall and creating the mushroom farm.

When I first lived in sharehouses I took it personally when people moved out but I was past this stage when Jerry left in a blaze of limp glory. I was equally nonplussed by who moved in. Blaze's real name was Craig and everyone called him Craig, apart from Craig, who called himself Blaze. He was the lead singer of a five-piece originals band whose sound was best described as shit. When everyone was embracing grunge or indie pop he was still happy pumping out eighties-style hard rock. He had long brown hair that he kept in a pony tail and almost always wore a leather vest without a shirt. He carried around a notebook he said was full of poetry, but the only thing I ever saw in it were his dole forms. He'd ploughed all his savings into a self-released album, which had attracted one review that began "I've never eaten dog's anus but I can only imagine it would be more pleasurable than listening to this record". What made Craig so fantastic is that the review didn't stop him doing what he loved. Seeing his band play in front of twelve people was glorious because Craig performed as if he was playing at Madison Square Garden. At the launch of their album they broke their own crowd record of twenty-one payers (they managed twenty-three) and he swanned around pre-gig in a robe with a glass of champagne in hand. Fifteen minutes before showtime he ducked upstairs to 'freshen up'. The rest of his band came on stage and started some sort of art rock prologue that went for the longest five minutes of our lives. Then everything went black and Craig burst on stage waving a dolphin torch like a search light, screaming into the microphone, "It's Blaze time!" For half the audience this signalled home time but he soldiered on as the lights came up to reveal him shirtless and wearing two pairs of black pantyhose that he was trying to pass off as Van Halen-style Spandex.

Craig hit his peak on the night we had a house party. Very early in the evening he decided to drop something that made him a hundred and fifty percent more Blaze. We had filled the bathtub with ice for drinks and at around 10:30pm he decided to get in, completely nude. If it wasn't bad enough that we had to reach between his legs to get a beer, he also refused to get out when the girls came in to go to the toilet. He compromised by putting a washer over his eyes but his head was still less than half a metre away from where they were having a wee. Not long after the party he moved in with his elderly grandmother to take the carer's benefit from the government and then got his Mum to do all the work.

At this stage my other housemate Stacey decided that we should get a girl to move in. Stacey was a non-identical twin who hated her sister. She was obsessed with the fact that they were both adopted and brought up as twins. Every time she got pissed she would finish each conversation with "I'm getting a DNA test to prove it," and the next morning she would do nothing. Stacey couldn't walk into a room without lighting incense and used to regularly make a pasta dish that consisted of fettuccine with tomato paste and steamed carrot, which was so delicious I could never finish it. She was permanently single so she got a puppy as a boyfriend substitute. Like all puppies, it was cute, but it grew up to be one of those annoying dogs that pissed on the carpet when anyone spoke. She took it to some hippy festival in the bush and said that someone stole him. Everyone thought she left him behind on purpose.

Her dreams of having a bestie to watch *Melrose Place* with were short-lived when Stuey moved in. We'd been without someone in the front room for all of three days and that was enough to push my finances to the limit so when we met Stuey through some friends I gave him a key straight away. He had been in between houses and put his single bed in the laundry of a friend's place and ended up staying there two years. He had developed quite severe allergy symptoms and when he told his GP he was living in a laundry the GP surmised the cause might be the OMO washing powder. It was probably the right diagnosis because after he moved in to a normal bedroom in our place his eyes stopped watering.

Stuey had spent the enrolment money that his Mum gave him for second-year uni at the pub and decided he'd just rock up to any classes he thought were interesting, even though he wasn't enrolled. He was paranoid about his Mum finding out so we weren't allowed to make small talk when she called on the phone in case we let something slip. When his folks went overseas for a month he was in charge of house-sitting and we all moved into their mansion in Kew. For just over three weeks we swam in the pool and ate and drank anything we could find in the house. I particularly enjoyed finding the spare keys to his Mum's Mercedes in a drawer and driving the car to university.

During the last few days in the mansion I noticed Stacey laughing at Stuey's particularly lame jokes. Then when we sadly went back to the terrace and I had to leave the Merc behind, I caught Stuey making positive comments about her fettuccine dish. Two nights later I came home late from a gig and Stuey's room was empty, door wide open and the light on. As I walked down the hallway I could hear Jeff Buckley's *Grace* coming out of her room.

HANIMEX
HANIMEX
tele
RICOH
126-C
EE
RIKENON
RICOH CO. LTD.
RICOH

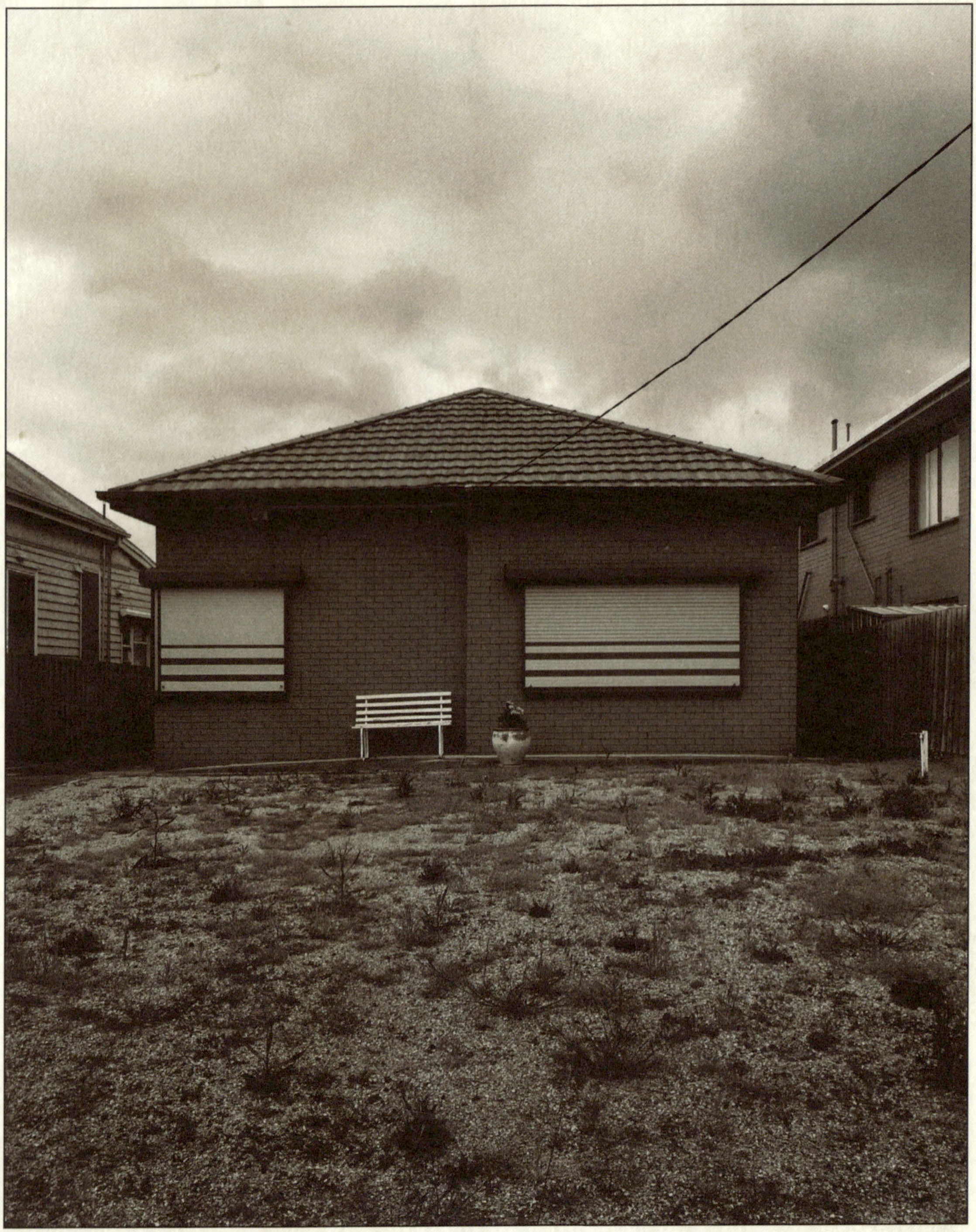

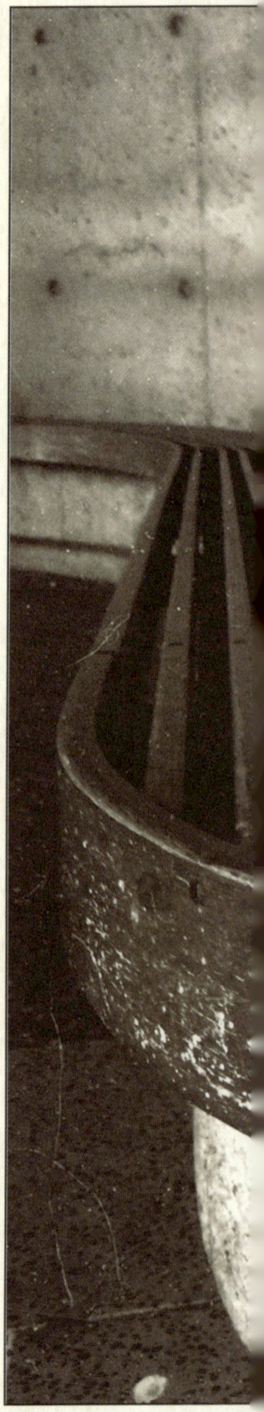

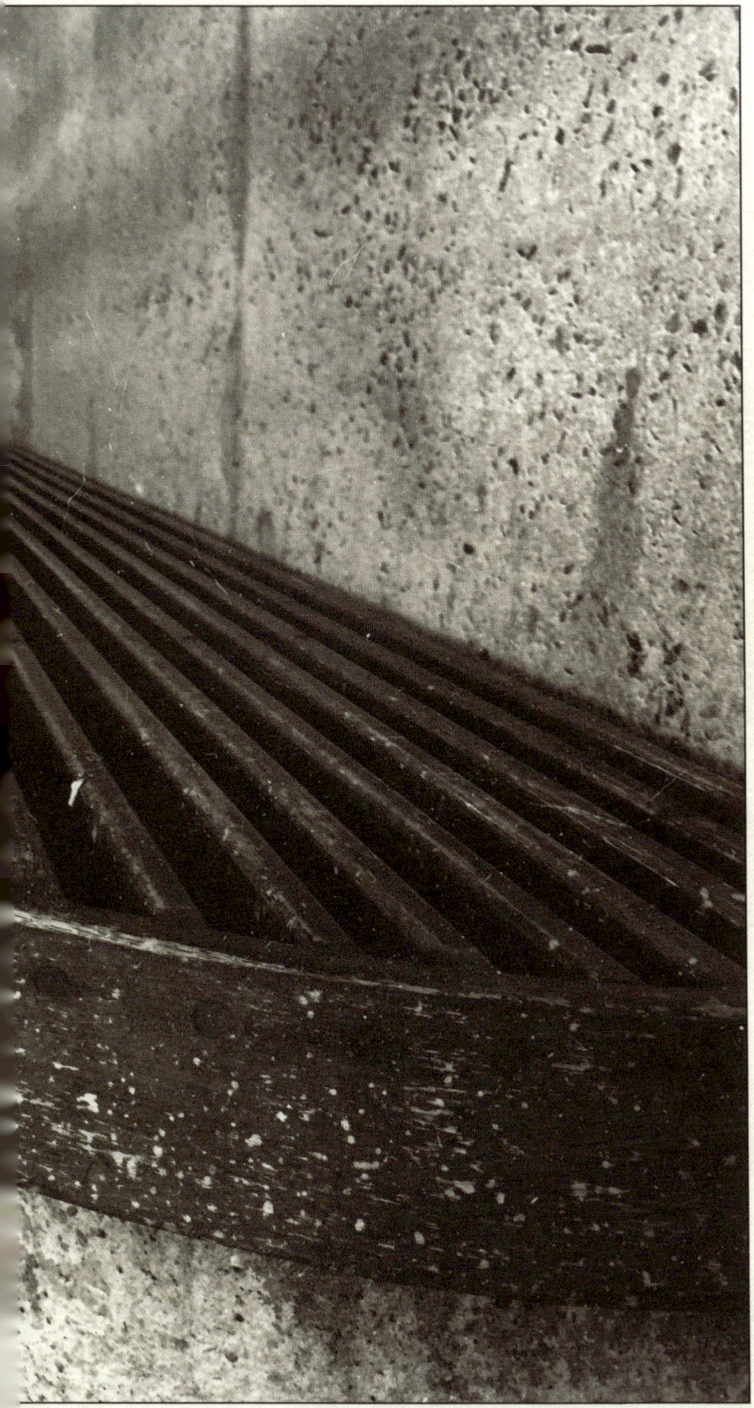

CHAPTER 14

The Last Pav

The last time Dane had been to the house there had been an almighty shit storm over a pavlova. He'd pulled into his old street and it was exactly the same dull slice of suburbia it had always been. Rows of Holdens and Toyotas and rows of wheelie bins with their flippy flappy lids of yellow, red and green. The flowering gums were always the same height; as soon as they got interesting the electricity company hacked them with a chainsaw and fed them into a machine that turned them into roundabout carpet.

He was cranky from the flight and cranky from hearing some song on the radio where a girl was in love with her own arse. Mentally his head was banging itself against the steering wheel of the tinny hire car. The house in Bexley looked the same. His Dad had clad it in faux weatherboard, well after anyone thought it was a good idea. As far as he was concerned, he'd had the last laugh because it had been ten years without painting it and "it still looked a treat". It was as yellow as it looked when he first saw the ad on TV where a footy hit the side of a house without marking it and a woman with a perm and Mersyndol-glazed eyes threw her husband's paint brushes in a bin that had a foot pedal-operated lid.

The salesman from Cronulla had also talked them into spray painting the tiled roof orange to "protect it for another 100 years", which is well beyond the time span that any sane person is concerned about their roof. The contractors who did the wall may have done a good job but the roof still looked like it was covered in fake tan and the large palm on the left hand side of the house had a massive orange blob on the trunk from a rather impressive mis-spray. His Dad had gone crook at the tradesman and to placate him the salesman gave him a book of vouchers featuring bargains like fifty percent off a game of Laser Tag at a shopping centre in Wollongong. His Dad didn't know what Laser Tag was but was happy to take the vouchers.

Dane had no illusions that returning for that Christmas was going to be like one of those American movies where everyone is initially excited to see each other and it's all hugs and playful ruffling of each other's hair. Then over the next hour and a half it slowly unravels and everyone takes it in turns to character assassinate each family member and explain how they ruined their lives.

That wasn't even close to how they rolled. Instead, Dane's family preferred to take their annual holiday at Ambivalence World. His Mum would be just interested enough to avoid seeming rude and then hover in the kitchen to avoid further conversation. His Dad would nod like he was listening but in reality would be waiting for a gap in the conversation so he could talk about something he had bought at Bunnings. As for his sister, she'd dial up the smile just long enough to cover her for five minutes after lunch, when she would make an excuse to leave. The smile would unravel as soon as she waved goodbye from her car and escaped down the street.

That year, the shit storm all started over a can of fruit. Ten minutes into standing around the kitchen drinking cheap sparkling,

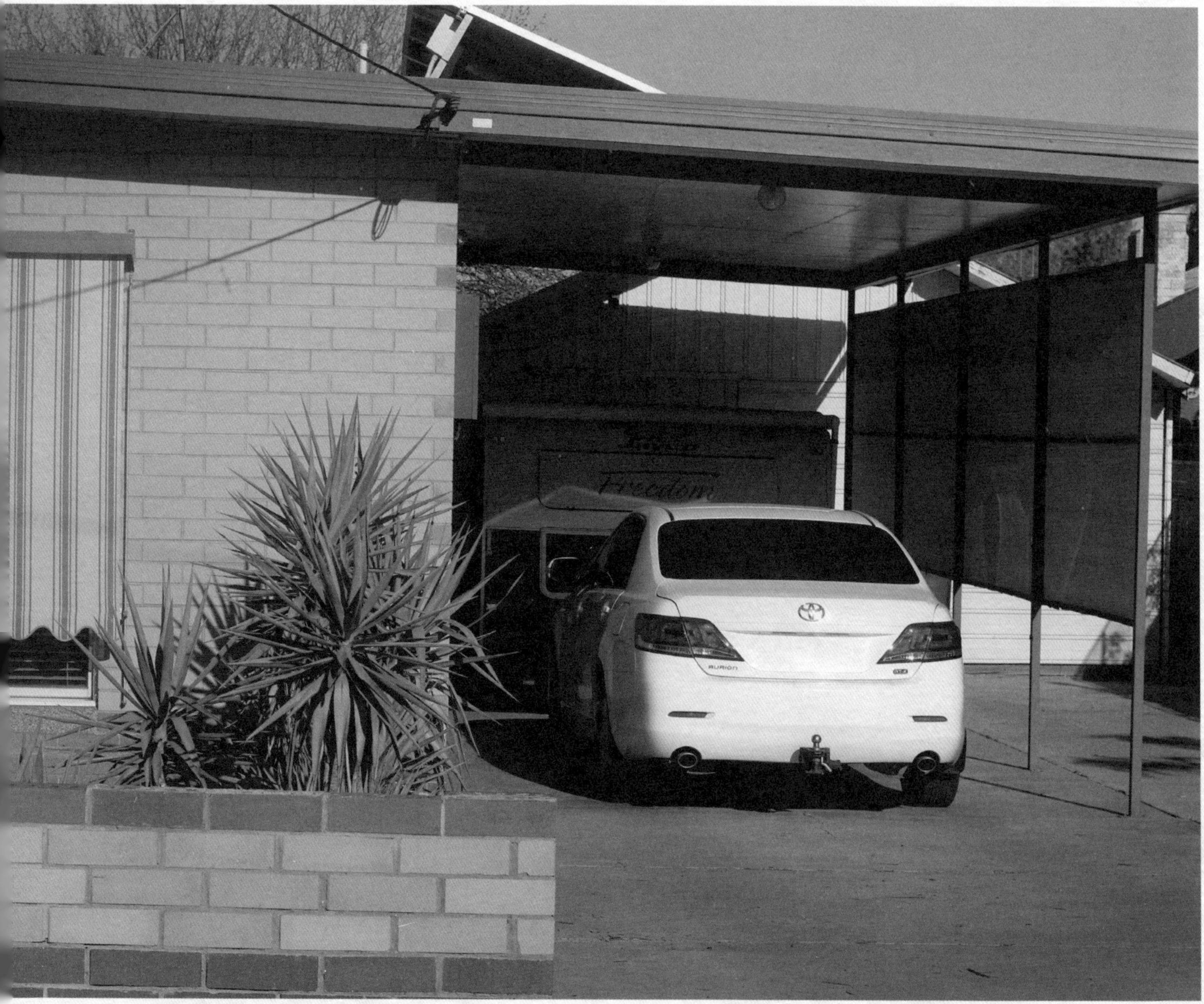
Freedom
AURION

his Mum started putting cream on the pav. She always made a pav because that's what she did, and everyone ate the pav because that's what they did. She always put it on a large orange plate that had brown patterned circles around the edge. It fit perfectly into a green Tupperware container every alternative year when it would travel along with the family to Uncle Ron's. The cream was going on with a plastic spatula when his sister picked up the tin of passionfruit.

"Mum, the fruit market is full of fresh passionfruit and you use this shit? What's wrong with using fresh fruit? Think about the food miles that have gone into processing this garbage". She paused and read the label. "Oh for fuck's sake! It's from Thailand and it's full of sugar!"

His sister used be a suburban netball queen. All her friends would zip around in their hatchbacks, meet for cappuccinos and focaccias, save for trips to Bali and have the same haircut. When she returned from Melbourne, she moved to Bondi, decided to get healthy and cut out everything, including being interesting. She'd racked up five years without eating pizza, which Dane thought seemed like a punishment rather than an achievement. Despite the yoga classes and the constant trendy health tonics she smashed, she wasn't any happier. She spent most of her time being paranoid about not being healthy enough. This wasn't helped by her 'health slip-ups', otherwise known as benders, where someone would dangle a bag and she would end up snorting the rent money off a cistern in the dunny of a bar full of people that made her feel old. The next day she would wake full of regrets. Every one of her nerve endings was a victim of the night before and she would drag herself sobbing to the beach for a run, picking the coke scabs in her nasal passages while she tried in vain to sprint herself happy.

Dane's Mum wasn't really seeing what the issue was.

"It's so much easier to get it on special from Woolies and leave it in the cupboard and use it when I'm ready."

"We live in a country with some of the best fruit in the world and everything is in season Mum, and you buy this shit in tins. I can't believe we grew up eating this rubbish — white bread sandwiches, processed everything. It's no wonder we were always sick. You've been trying to poison us our whole lives."

Dane decided to get involved.

"I liked tomato sauce sandwiches and I've never been sick."

"This family is fucked!"

She stormed out, slamming the flyscreen door.

"She needs a boyfriend," his Mum mumbled as she spooned the last bit of passionfruit on top of the pav.

Nobody agreed or added anything. They had lunch and his Mum listed all the people he had gone to school with that she'd bumped into at the supermarket. By the time they'd had a slice of pav his Dad was sitting on his recliner with the dog on his lap watching TV. He didn't get up when Dane left, barely mumbled goodbye. His Mum hugged him lightly and gave him a piece of pav wrapped in wax paper inside a takeaway container. He'd been in the house for less than two hours.

He didn't text his sister. It didn't even occur to him. At the airport he couldn't cope with the weirdness of putting a piece of pav through the X-ray machine so he lobbed it into the bin. He couldn't wait to get on the plane back to Perth.

That had been a year ago and here he was again going through the flyscreen door and down the hallway where his Dad once again was sitting on his chair with the dog on his lap. His sister was in the kitchen putting things in boxes and they silently embraced. His Dad didn't get up.

"Much traffic from the airport son?"

"Was pretty good actually Dad. What's the score?"

The merits of the new opening combination were briefly discussed and then he joined his sister in the kitchen. She put a crystal vase to one side with a post-it note with her name on it. The light brown bowls he had eaten cereal-with-two-fruits in as a kid were wrapped roughly in newspaper and put in a box for the op shop. Dane picked up the orange plate with the brown patterns on it and added to the box.

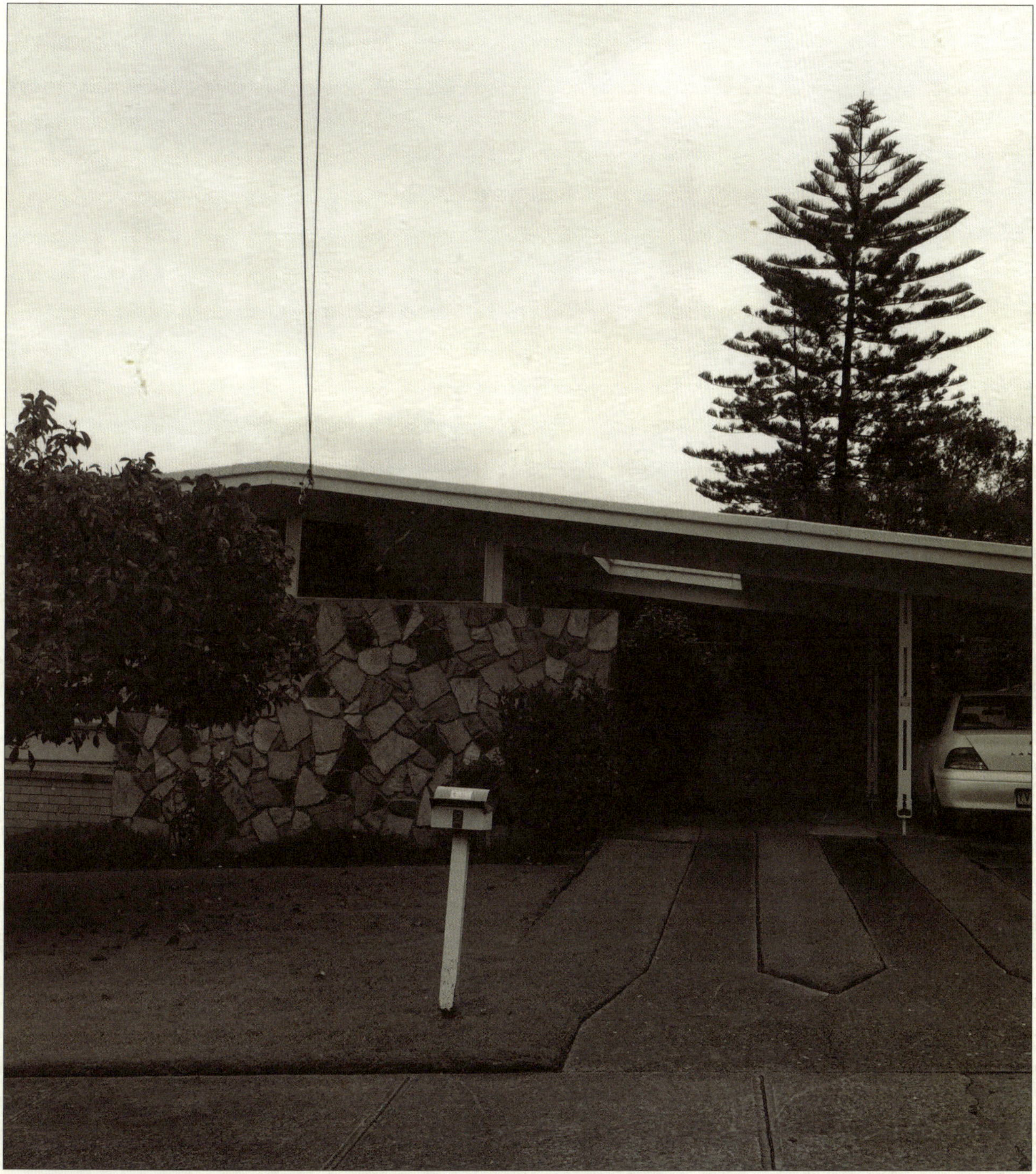

CHAPTER 15

Good Night

Dad was limping around my house exactly like a seventy-nine year old man who'd had a couple of hip replacements should. It was September in Sydney and he was being typically Melbourne, wearing a V-neck woollen jumper even though it was twenty-six degrees outside. He was on his second cup of tea and had pulled an obscure book out of the shelf and was devouring it voraciously. He sat with his legs crossed and the chair on a forty-five degree angle with his right elbow resting on the table, the exact same position I remember him sitting in at the kitchen table in my childhood house.

He'd arrived at Melbourne airport a good four hours before his domestic flight just to be certain that he was four hours early. When I pulled in to pick him up in Sydney, I looked down at my hands gripping the steering wheel and noticed how much they looked like his. One Sunday when I was five, I was holding on to his hand after church. I remember running my fingers over the ridge of his wedding ring and then grabbing his pointer finger and swinging from side to side on my heels. His hand felt so big and safe and I kept swinging further and further out until I lost grip momentarily. I reached out and found his hands again, grabbed hold and went back to swinging. When I finally got bored and stopped, I looked up and I was no longer holding on to Dad's hand, but his friend's who he was standing next to; when I had let go I had grabbed his by mistake. As I realised what had happened, I burst into tears.

These were the hands that Uncle Jim, my mum's brother, credits with bringing a warmth and tactility to a family that wasn't big on the hug until Dad came along and married his sister. Physicality didn't just come easy to Dad, it's who he is. He can't have a conversation without reaching out and touching a hand, forearm or elbow.

My hands today are of the same vintage as when he sat with me on the carpet in the living room and we made things together out of Meccano, and when he got a large piece of plywood and made a city for my Matchbox cars. He built buildings out of polystyrene, covered them in sticking plaster and painstakingly painted them. My favourite was the hospital that had a red cross painted on the helipad roof. He collected sea sponges from the beach, painted them green and fashioned them into mini trees using copper wire for the trunks.

They are the hands that swung me around when he picked me up from preschool on the days we walked home rather than drove. When it was just the two of us and we stopped to look at the different birds in the large gums and he taught me how to identify the animals that had been around based on their turds. These were the hands that made illustrated books that went with the fantastical tales he made up and told me as bedtime stories. I loved how he crawled into bed next to me and created vivid images in my mind and characters that jumped to life and became real. Some nights when he finished the story he'd lay there exhausted from a big day at work and fall asleep before me. I'd watch his chest rise and fall and wait for the snoring to kick in.

When Dad tries to read to him, my four-year-old Bugsy does everything to distract him. He jumps on his lap and squeezes his nose like a horn until Dad takes the hint and starts entertaining him with a Darth Vader voice that sounds nothing like Darth Vader but has Bugsy in hysterics. Now he has him captive, he drags him off to his room to torture him with tales of Lego-making. Bugsy's little hands grab the hands that are now creased and shake, but still radiate the same kindness and warmth.

Later that night, after half bits of pasta twirls have been scattered across the kitchen bench and little nude bodies have jumped on our bed trying to avoid pyjamas and combs, the two little people are finally wrangled. Dad lies with Bugsy and tells him the stories he used to tell me when I was his age. I go to get the camera and by the time I return they are both fast asleep.

The Rumpus Room
and other stories from the suburbs.

Tim Ross   **Wanker author shot.**